MARY E. STIBAL

A SISTER IN RUBIES

A Gemstone Mystery

I dedicate A Sister in Rubies to Shay Morton, my very real older sister, who is a wonderful, brilliant, and caring sister, and yes, prettier, too! I love you, Shay.

Praise for A Sister in Rubies

"*A Sister in Rubies* is another great addition to the Gemstone Mystery Series. Loosely based on the real theft from the Duchess of Windsor in the UK, this book is an edgy, thrilling read."—Mary Buckham, *USA Today* bestselling author

Chapter One

Sunningdale, UK

The readers of the local newspapers in Sunningdale were aware the anniversary of the famous jewelry theft from the Duchess of Windsor was coming up in October. Every year the local media never failed to remind their readers of that story, as if they might have forgotten.

For the last several weeks nine people had been scrutinizing *The Bracknell Times* and *The Ascot and Eaton Express*, alert for the slightest reference to any update on the unsolved, eighty-year-old burglary.

Six were true-crime aficionados, the over-educated, tedious kind. The remaining three could be classified as obsessed, the type that never give up. They watched and read the news carefully because there was still much at stake.

Ascot, UK

A long-time Patron of the public library in Ascot and one of its top donors sat at a table in the Reading Room. The Patron wasn't interested in reading any biographies of the Duchess of Windsor; that information was old and had already been examined. After hanging a black cashmere scarf on the back of the chair, the Patron turned to one of the library's computers, the afternoon sun glinting off the solid gold Rolex watch strapped around the

Patron's wrist.

With a sigh, the Patron logged into the library's periodical database and clacked "Theft of the Duchess of Windsor's Jewelry in Sunningdale, UK" in the search bar in case something new had surfaced.

The Patron was a believer in constant vigilance.

The lights abruptly came on in the hall as someone walked down the stairs and passed by the Reading Room. Two minutes later, the lights were flicked off, and the slam of a door from downstairs drifted up the steps. Silence. The visitor, whoever it was, had left. The Patron relaxed.

There was no choice but to continue the hunt for new information. The Patron needed to beat pesky amateur sleuths to the solution of the old crime. They were the only real danger because the public wasn't all that interested in the old crime.

The Patron opened the first string of links but saw nothing new and then went through the next fifty. Still nothing. The Patron continued to scroll, opening all of them, just in case.

For years, it had seemed that the stolen jewelry would stay lost for eternity, which was just fine with the Patron. Perfect, in fact, given the situation. Still, although interest had waned, it was still there, bubbling up every now and then like swamp gas. The problem was someone could still find the case of stolen jewelry because it was out there, somewhere.

If the jewelry collection was found, there was the possibility that a thorough investigation of the old crime would be launched, with old reputations ruined and an ancient institution forever scarred, if it survived. The Patron had to stop that from ever happening.

Ten minutes later, the Patron spotted something unusual, something unexpected, in a fragment of an old article that had focused on an officer involved in Scotland Yard's investigation of the theft. It was only a couple of sentences, taken from an article published in 1947, a year after the burglary, in a British tabloid. The tabloid had long since folded, but the fragment had unfortunately survived and had just resurfaced. The Patron read it five times because it contained an unmistakable clue that, even after all these years, could blow everything open. Wide open.

An hour later the Patron headed down the stairs to the lobby, pulling up the hood of a thick jacket as the sound of a sudden rain hammered against the windows. The head librarian, Kathleen, a striking-looking blonde, her reading glasses a glamorous red, called out from her desk, "It was good to see you again. Goodbye, have a nice night, and stay dry."

The Patron replied with a nod of the head and walked out the door into the rain. The three-hour visit to the library had been worth it. The posthumous awarding of the medal of the Royal Victorian Order should never have been published in any newspaper in 1947. Someone had let that slip by years ago. In fact, however, the medal should never have been awarded by George VI in the first place because it raised the specter of a connection between the burglary and Buckingham Palace.

It was a miracle no one had picked up on it at the time.

* * *

Once Kathleen heard the front door slam shut behind the Patron, she clicked on the computer at her desk and scrolled through the long string of articles the Patron had just opened. The librarian was aware the anniversary of the Windsor theft was approaching, but why did the Patron have such a focused interest? Kathleen had always been curious about the crime, not so much because it had been local, but because it was mysterious, like the rich and powerful Patron.

It took Kathleen almost half an hour to print off copies of the articles the Patron had opened on the library's computer. She skimmed the pages during the slow afternoon, stopping only once, surprised by what she read. She picked up a thick black pen and scrawled a question mark and the word "Why?" in thick black ink on the page and then underlined the word three times with her pen. She would follow up on that because the timing of the award struck her as unusual, even odd. Kathleen turned down the corner of the page.

She knew it would take her at least a week, maybe even a bit longer, to find the answer, since it would involve digging through old, archived files in the library basement, but she would make the time. By now she was more than just a little curious, Kathleen knew enough that she was suspicious.

After she re-shelved a pile of returned books, Kathleen slid her stack of copies in a heavy canvas bag, her favorite, with an outline of the UK studded in red Swarovski crystals. She set her canvas bag by the front door to take home at 6:00.

* * *

An hour later, the Patron realized their expensive, black cashmere scarf was still on a chair in the Reading Room, so the Patron returned to the library in the rain. The librarian was not at her desk when the Patron slipped up the stairs to the Reading Room, picked up the scarf, and returned to the main floor. On the way out, the Patron accidentally knocked over Kathleen's canvas bag of copies by the front door.

Several pages spilled out of the bag, and after a look at the pages and then a glance inside, the Patron realized she had copied the articles they had opened just two hours before. All of them, every one of them. The Patron sifted through the pages, one ear bent for any footfalls on the stairs above, and abruptly stopped at a page with the corner turned down. Someone had scrawled the word "Why?" in black ink and heavily underlined it three times. A comment the Patron knew hadn't been on the original two hours earlier.

Then the Patron heard the squeak of a step on the stair and slid the pages back in the bag.

Patron opened the front door and left. Someone, and it could only have been Kathleen, the librarian, had flagged the mention of the Royal Victorian Order awarded so many years ago with one scrawled underlined word, "Why?"

The Patron knew why.

The Patron also knew there was only one way to solve the problem of the librarian and her unfortunate curiosity because she was now a very real danger. Something would need to be done, and it would need to look like an accident, of course, just another unfortunate, fatal accident.

Boston

The next morning Madeline Lane, co-owner of Coda Gems, a high-end jewelry store on the expensive end of Boston's Newbury Street, double-checked their four cut-glass display cases one last time. The jewelry, all by luxury brands that included Cartier, Tiffany, and Harry Winston, gleamed under the $12,000 LED spotlights they'd bought three years ago. Now, Madeline wished they hadn't spent that kind of money on lighting.

She glanced in a mirror and ran a comb through her short, curly blonde hair one more time. As usual, Madeline wore a cashmere tunic, black designer jeans, and cowboy boots; today's were her favorite, custom-made and a pale yellow.

She straightened the dark brown leather and rattan bar stools scattered along the display cases, and watered their one plant, a tall sago palm that was either doing just all right or was about to die, it was hard to tell which. On the walls, in matte black frames, hung prints of Boston Symphony seasons from 1931–1939, which Madeline bought because she thought it gave the store an air of 'Old Money'.

She walked over to the display case that held their ruby and diamond jewelry and picked up a five-carat Cartier ruby ring. The day before Coda Gems had placed an ad in *The Boston Globe* announcing a special sale, and this ring should be included. Taking a red pen Madeline drew a line through the $36,000 price, and scrawled $25,000 above it, an insanely good price for the ring, but they needed the money.

Madeline thought about frog-marching customers over to try it on once the store opened, which almost made her laugh. Abby, her business partner, was a stickler about any number of things, which no doubt included felony assault. However, that one sale wouldn't fix their problem; COVID-19 and its financial impact had been a sad monkey wrench for the store. The store was in financial trouble, big trouble.

A minute later Abby walked in the door and Madeline didn't need to look at her watch, it would be exactly 9:45 am. Abby was nothing if not precise, an excellent quality since she was the CFO as well as the co-owner of Coda Gems. Abby's glossy black hair was pulled back in a French braid, her dark bangs sensible. She wore no earrings that day and, no surprise, her Armani suit was blue, this one a dark navy.

Abby hung her jacket in the back closet and set a brown bag with her lunch in their small refrigerator: a salad with brie cheese, leeks, kale, of course, olive oil, and possibly raisins.

"Did you see our ad in *The Globe* this morning?" said Abby, and handed Madeline a copy of the newspaper, folded to Coda Gems' four-color ad. Abby was proud of the ad, since she'd designed it herself.

"Yes, I saw it. It's beautiful, and on page three, no less. I hope it works," said Madeline.

The headline above the four-color photo of a glittering jumble of emerald, diamond, and ruby bracelets and rings read, 'Give Yourself Something Extraordinary! Select Jewelry up to 50% off!"

"Just in case the ad doesn't work," said Madeline, "it might make sense to hire someone wearing a sandwich board to parade up and down in front of our store for a week or two," which she thought was funny, but Abby didn't appreciate the remark. Madeline should have known better; Abby was a great business partner, but she had no sense of humor when it came to money.

Madeline glanced at their ad again and guessed they had wasted their money. An expensive, but run-of-the-mill print ad wouldn't be enough to save their business. What they needed was a new, bold idea to bring in new customers; a glossy ad wouldn't change anything.

On top of that worry, Madeline's older sister, Shay, was coming to stay with her in Boston for a whole week, a visit that Madeline didn't have time for, not now, with Coda Gems on the verge of going out of business. She wished Shay wasn't coming to Boston; the timing could not have been worse.

"What does Felix think of our ad?" said Abby.

Felix was Madeline's ex-husband who was a reporter at *The Boston Globe*.

He was also the helpful type, as far as ex-husbands go.

"I don't know if he's seen it," said Madeline, "I think he's been out of town or something. I'm sure he'll call me when he sees it."

"The ad has to work because..." began Abby, her voice trailing off.

"Because what?" asked Madeline, but Abby didn't respond, and Madeline didn't press her.

Finally, Abby said, "Business could be better, a lot better. But then you know what I think we should do about that."

Madeline knew very well what Abby wanted to do, and she didn't say anything.

"It's just that the rent here is killing us," added Abby.

Which was partly Madeline's fault, since she had talked Abby into relocating the store to the upscale and very expensive Newbury Street three years before. Madeline sighed. Moving their store to the upscale street had been a brilliant idea. At the time.

* * *

Madeline's sister Shay, an interior design photographer in San Francisco, called her that evening. "I have some good news and some bad news," she began.

"I just picked up a new client, a ritzy golf club in the UK, the Sunningdale Golf Club. The creative director there is an old friend of mine from Boston, and he is desperate because he just lost his photographer. He wants me to fly to the UK for a photoshoot, and I need to call him tomorrow and let him know if I can help him out. The trouble is, it's a five-day photoshoot and is right in the middle of my trip to see you in Boston, and I..."

"Don't worry about that," said Madeline quickly, "we can postpone your visit, no problem. We'll just get together another time. It will be fine. Besides, a couple of things have come up here and I..."

"No, no, I really want to come and see you; after all, we've been planning this for months. I'll turn down the photo shoot."

"Will it pay well?" asked Madeline.

"Well…" said Shay, "in a word, yes."

"Then don't be ridiculous," said Madeline, "do not, I repeat, do not, turn it down. You should go, and besides, it sounds glamorous."

"Glamorous? Hardly. The town is tiny, with a population of about seven thousand, and it's twenty-five miles outside of London in the middle of nowhere," Shay laughed, "so there's plenty of room for expensive, 18-hole golf courses. The golf club is about to finish a multi-million-dollar renovation of its clubhouse and guest rooms, so they need stunning interior photos. That's why Chip wants me to fly in, but Madeline, I'd much rather come and see you in Boston. If I take this photo gig, I'll end up spending most of my time thousands of miles away in a pokey little town I've never heard of."

"What's the name of this 'pokey little town'?" asked Madeline.

"Sunningdale."

"Sunningdale? That's funny. I have heard of it," said Madeline. "It's famous in the jewelry world because there was a big burglary, or a supposed burglary, there a long time ago. A fortune in high-end jewelry was stolen from the Duchess of Windsor, and then the jewelry collection disappeared off the face of the earth. No one ever found out what happened to it. But Shay, I think you should go to the UK for the photoshoot instead of coming to Boston. Seriously, you should go."

There was a long silence before Shay said, "Here's a thought Madeline, why don't you just come with me to Sunningdale for the photoshoot? It would be fun."

"What? No, I can't, not now, it's just impossible, totally impossible. I am sorry, but I am up my neck with problems here at the store, big ones, so I just can't leave now."

"I guess I probably should just go to the photo shoot and…" sighed Shay and stopped. "Why don't I get a multi-stop ticket, fly to Boston, stay with you for three days instead of seven, and then fly to the UK for the photo shoot?" she pressed. "It's better than just postponing my visit. Again."

"Well…" Madeline finally said, "Yes, I guess that could work, I suppose it would be alright. But I will have to go to the store a couple of times while you are in Boston, it just can't be helped because…"

"No problem, I understand. I'll book my flights this afternoon and text you the info. Tell me, how are you, and how are things at Coda Gems?"

"It's a bit slow now," said Madeline, "but Abby and I are coming up with ideas."

Madeline didn't mention that Abby had already come up with a big one two weeks before. Abby had said they had no choice; they had to seriously consider selling Coda Gems to an interested buyer, a chain of national jewelry stores based in California.

Madeline had had a four-word response to Abby's idea, and she had muttered, "Over my dead body."

Abby had pretended she hadn't heard.

* * *

The next day, Madeline was about to leave Grill 23 in downtown Boston after lunch with a New York gem dealer when she saw her ex-husband, Felix, a tall, lean man in his mid-thirties, his long blonde hair combed straight back, sitting at a table in the back. When Felix noticed her, he stood up abruptly from his chair and wound his way up to her.

Felix was in blue jeans, a long-sleeved white shirt, and a leather jacket, his standard work attire, and he kissed Madeline on the cheek, "Fancy running into you here, of all places in Boston. I am surprised to see you."

"You make it sound as if this is an opium den or something," she said.

After their divorce four years ago, Madeline had been bitter, but Felix was just sad, and he'd left his job as a reporter at *The Boston Globe's* award-winning investigative news unit, *Spotlight*, and moved to Chicago as a reporter at *The Chicago Sun*. Then a year and a half ago he had come back to *The Boston Globe* and to his old *Spotlight* team, this time as a Senior Investigative Reporter.

After he'd moved back Felix wanted to see Madeline again, the lunch or just-drinks kind of seeing each other she thought. At first, she hadn't been interested, but then she decided 'why not'? Felix had helped her out from time to time with information she needed for her customers at Coda Gems. The man did know everyone in Boston, and apparently the entire country;

she'd seen his cellphone bills.

"Got a minute?" Felix said that afternoon as he looked around the restaurant, and he nodded at an empty table, and they sat down.

"I am glad to see you because I was going to call you tonight," he said with a slow smile. "I've just accepted a new position at *The Globe*. I am now officially the new managing editor of *Spotlight*! I'll be the *de facto* leader of the whole investigative news unit now, the head honcho, 'the Man.'"

Madeline wasn't surprised, she was astonished, and not in a good way.

"I guess investigative reporting is in my blood," he said.

Madeline hadn't replied, she'd just sat silent, not looking at him. It wasn't in her blood.

"It will be different this time," he said, in his 'I really mean this' tone. "I won't be a reporter anymore; I'll be the one in charge. I am working on a story now for my series on liquefied natural gas tankers in Boston, but I'll be finished with that in a month, and then I'll become just another plain old boring, executive head of *Spotlight*. Maybe I'll even start wearing suspenders." Felix paused for a couple of seconds, and laughed, "Well no, I won't do that. But it will be different this time, totally different, you'll see."

She looked at him then out of the corner of her eye. Who was he kidding? But why did it matter to her? They were no longer married, and they were certainly not in an intimate relationship. She was glad they weren't.

"Well then, congratulations are in order, and I am happy for you."

She knew Felix would become totally absorbed 24/7 in whatever story the *Spotlight* team had identified as critical, a story that usually involved the rich and their abuse of power. Investigative reporters are a breed apart in the news world since they have the luxury of time to focus on a critical and usually complex story. They are also relentless, and Felix was one of the best. He had won two Pulitzer Prizes for investigative reporting, and Madeline suspected he was gunning for a third. Felix's job had been the primary reason she had filed for divorce.

It wasn't true that that Felix's career always came first, what was true was that he was obsessed with the investigation part, and he did have a hunger for justice.

What Felix loved more than anything was to be on the hunt.

* * *

Several days later, Madeline's sister Shay arrived from San Francisco on a late-night flight that was two hours late, and to make matters worse, the two sisters stayed up playing gin rummy, and Shay won every hand, as usual.

Madeline slept through the alarm on her cell phone the next morning, so it was 9:15 by the time she rushed into Coda Gems, but she didn't need to worry. Abby had already set up the jewelry displays.

"I got your text that you'd be late, so I took care of setting up the displays," said Abby and handed Madeline a cup of steaming coffee.

"Thanks. These days, it seems a lot of planes are late or cancelled."

"Unfortunately, that's true," said Abby. "It's fine though, it's not as if we have customers lined up outside our door. You must be glad to have Shay here in Boston."

"I am glad, very glad, but she's not staying very long, just a couple of days," and Madeline glanced at the calendar on her desk. "She lives so far away, and I miss her, even if she does drive me crazy," and Madeline quickly added, "from time to time."

Shay was six years older than Madeline, but it could have been six decades. They were opposites, and about the only thing the two had in common was that their parents were the same people. Shay was also very stubborn, the inflexible kind of stubborn.

Growing up, Shay had no time for an adoring younger sister who followed her around like a short, pudgy shadow. When she was eighteen, Shay wore only cowboy boots, so Madeline did too, which she continued to wear even after Shay moved on to elegant ballet slippers, black ones, edged with gold.

However, the critical difference between them was that Madeline was a pragmatist, while Shay was a hard-core romantic, the kind with an unshakeable, bordering-on-fanatic belief in love and happy endings. Madeline had no idea where in the world that came from. It was as if Shay had been radicalized by the Hallmark Channel.

* * *

That morning, after Abby asked Madeline how Shay's flight had been, other than delayed, she went straight to her desk in the back and got on the phone. For the last ten months Abby's desk had been stacked with financial spread sheets and applications for bank loans, "to tide us over until the economy really picks up," she'd told Madeline.

Thirty minutes later, as Madeline made a couple of minor adjustments to the emerald and then the sapphire display cases, she could hear Abby at her desk, still on the phone, probably with a bank. They had been about to close on a $250,000 loan with a bank on Boston's South Shore the month before, but the bank had pulled the loan at the last minute. Shortly after, Neptune Diamonds, a big jewelry store chain based in California, had let Abby know they were interested in buying Coda Gems, and were she and her partner interested in selling?

Madeline never asked Abby in detail about Neptune's interest; she didn't want to talk about selling Coda Gems to any jewelry store chain, much less to a big and uninspired one like Neptune. She also thought Neptune was just fishing around, but Abby didn't. Abby was ready to sell.

At 10:00 a.m., Madeline could hear Abby still on her phone. She glanced at her watch; it was time to open the store. She double-checked each of their display cases one last time and walked over to the glass case that held their ruby jewelry. She picked up the Cartier ruby ring and admired the brilliant-cut stone again. It was a pity it hadn't sold, especially at the sale price. She had been so sure it would.

However, Madeline didn't put the ring back in the ruby display case. Instead, she walked to their cut glass case of diamond jewelry by the front door, moved five stacks of Tiffany diamond bracelets and necklaces to the side, and set the ruby ring on a black velvet display stand directly under three powerful spotlights. The effect of ruby red splinters of color against the black velvet was spectacular.

Madeline knew someone would fall in love with the ring, and the sooner, the better.

Five minutes later two customers walked in the door, and Madeline watched as they walked up to the glass case with the ruby ring and left a minute later. Suddenly she heard a low voice behind her, "Madeline, I've told you before your store is quite impressive; it is beautiful, and the location is perfect. You were smart to make the move to Newbury Street."

Madeline turned around and her sister Shay flashed a smile. Shay always had moved like a whisper, ballet slippers notwithstanding. She was quiet, too quiet, and over the years Madeline was used to Shay suddenly appearing out of thin air, which wasn't so much unsettling as it was just plain annoying.

Madeline's sister was four inches shorter than her, but prettier; she had long dark hair, and her eyes were a dreamy soft brown. Shay glanced around the store and adjusted the velvet cloak around her shoulders, her curling dark hair falling around her shoulders, her beige silk scarf long and flowing. She didn't look like a professional photographer, she looked like a 19th century British novelist, the kind who walked in misty mornings along sandy beaches, with the mournful sound of a foghorn forever in the distance. Like on TV.

Shay poured a cup of coffee and walked along their display cases. When she reached the glass case in the front, she stopped dead and stared at the five-carat ruby ring, the stone shimmering under their LED spotlights.

Shay said to Madeline over her shoulder, "That is an incredible ring Madeline, it is drop-dead gorgeous! I never realized before that rubies were so breathtaking." Shay looked up, "The ruby stone is just...well...it's mesmerizing. Could I try it on, just for a minute?"

Madeline walked over, pulled out her set of thirty-plus keys from a chain on her belt and slid one into the lock of the glass case. She handed the ruby ring to Shay who studied it, then flipped over the price tag for the price, and said, "If you die tomorrow, can I have this?"

A constant question from their childhood, which had been funny when they were young, not so funny now that they were both middle-aged. Then Madeline thought about it for a second; no, it was even funnier now.

"You can absolutely have it," said Madeline. "Since you're the executor of my will, you can do what you want."

"Legally, no, I can't, but I'll take your word about the ring." She slipped the

13

five-carat ruby ring on her finger and stretched out her hand, admiring the facets of the red gemstone glittering the spotlights.

After a long minute, Shay took off the ring, and Madeline opened the case again with her jangling set of keys. Shay had told Madeline once that her heavy ring of clattering keys made her look and sound like a janitor. Madeline slid the ruby ring back under the brilliance of the three spotlights.

"I can't stay much longer," said Shay. "I needed to get out for a short walk, and I have to leave in about five minutes."

Madeline guessed she was heading back to her condo on Channel Center Street to work on one of her 'Save the Whales' projects. Shay was a certified scuba diver and shot underwater photos, pro bono, for three charities.

Shay walked along their display cases a second time scanning their jewelry, looking up at the front door every now and then. There were no customers in the store.

"You could do with a bit more business," said Shay. "In the last thirty-five minutes, no one, not a single customer, has walked in."

"Business is a shade above terrible," said Madeline, "and not what it used to be before COVID. We've tried advertising and promotions, but nothing has made a difference. I was keen on celebrity endorsements for about a minute, but the only famous people I admire are dead, so getting a compelling endorsement would be…unlikely."

Shay didn't laugh. Neither had Abby when she mentioned it a month ago.

"We've been going over our options," continued Madeline, "and lately, Abby says we need to consider selling Coda Gems, which is breaking my heart. I am not about to let this store…just cease to exist." She continued with a sad smile, "She and I will have to do something, something different, something big. We'll just have to come up with a miracle."

Madeline was lost in thought for a minute, staring down at the ruby ring, and then, with a big smile, she looked up at her sister, "You know what, Shay, I just had a brilliant idea, a good one." She paused thinking, then said, "It will be difficult, but yes, I believe it can work."

"I do have to ask," said Shay, "since you've been sounding a little desperate, is it legal? The last thing I need is a jailbird for a sister."

Madeline laughed, "Understood, but yes, it is totally legal."

"Good, just checking. Tell me, what is your fabulous brainstorm?"

"I think Abby and I should drop our focus on selling new jewelry pieces from the luxury brands, and instead we should concentrate on 'estate jewelry,'" said Madeline, warming up to her idea. "That's an elegant name, isn't it? In the gem business it means high-end, but previously owned jewelry. The margins would be better, a lot better so our prices would be lower, and business would be sure to pick up."

Shay smiled, "Yes, that does sound like a good plan, but you should somehow add in romance. Everyone wants a little romance in their life. Romance does make the world go around, you know."

Madeline said, "Shay, you are sadly mistaken; money is what makes the world go around."

"I do like the term 'estate jewelry,'" said Shay, "which sounds very upper class. Just add in romance."

Five minutes later, a customer came in, and after twenty minutes of examining their collection of 18 kt. jewelry with Madeline, he bought an 18-kt. gold Tiffany bracelet for $15,000.

"It's a twentieth anniversary present for my wonderful wife," he said as Madeline tied a gold ribbon around a Coda Gems' black velvet box and slipped it in a matte black bag for the man.

Shay watched the husband go out the door with his anniversary present, and she walked over and said to Madeline, "See, think romance and business will be better."

Madeline shrugged, "A nice thought, but romance won't pay the rent."

* * *

That night Madeline and Shay had dinner at Francesca's, an Italian restaurant in Boston's North End. The restaurant, like all restaurants in the North End it, was crowded with a mix of tourists and crusty Bostonians.

"I know I will dream of rubies tonight," said Shay, "A ruby ring would be perfect, because you can wear it every day, not like a necklace, or a brooch."

She laughed, "Or a tiara."

"Yes," said Madeline, "rings are great." Madeline never wore one, had never even worn a wedding ring when she was married, but she didn't mention that.

"I do love rings," said Shay, and she unconsciously twisted the heavy diamond wedding ring on her left hand. Shay had been married to Harrison, a lawyer, and the love of her life, and they'd lived in New York City. Then five years ago Harrison had been diagnosed with mesothelioma at Sloan Kettering and Shay took care of him in their co-op on the East Side until he took his last, sad breath. Right after that, Shay had moved to San Francisco and never spoke of him, but she hadn't taken off her wedding ring, a platinum band with three-and-a-half carats of class D diamonds.

The waiter poured Shay another glass of chardonnay as she said to Madeline, "Before the start of the photoshoot in Sunningdale, I will spend two or three days in London with Chip, their creative director, and I am looking forward to it. I think it would be great to live in London. All that history and..."

"And fog," said Madeline.

"Yes, that too. I like fog, I love fog, it's so mysterious and dreamy."

"And wet. Fog is wet, and it's cold as well," said Madeline.

"Don't be ridiculous. Fog is hauntingly beautiful and so romantic."

Madeline arched her eyebrows and picked up her wine glasses.

"It's time for a toast, don't you think?" said Shay. "I propose a toast to my future and to yours," said Shay. "May we both find romance, the forever kind."

"Now you sound like a TV commercial for an overpriced engagement ring," laughed Madeline.

"You've become jaded over the years, dear sister. Me? I want true love," said Shay, "and a ruby ring."

The sisters clinked wine glasses, and Madeline drained her glass. "Tell me, how did you get the Sunningdale photo gig in the first place?"

"Chip had a photographer from Paris under contract for almost three months to take the photos, but then her husband was hospitalized in

Cambodia and needed bypass surgery, so she had to cancel at the last minute. When Chip asked me to come, I told him I had a conflict, but I'd see what I could do to help him out."

"I can't believe you were thinking of turning it down," said Madeline.

Shay smiled and shrugged.

"You know what?" said Madeline, "while you're in Sunningdale, would you mind going past the scene of that theft from the Duchess of Windsor and take a couple of pictures for me? I am curious, since it was so famous, and so odd."

"Sure, send me the address, and I will do that. But what do you mean, odd? What was odd about the burglary?" said Shay.

"Odd? From what I remember," said Madeline, "pretty much everything."

* * *

The next morning, Madeline was at the store until Noon, then picked up Shay and drove fifteen miles down to Hull, a small town on the Atlantic. They walked along the roiling ocean on Nantasket Beach for ten minutes until they reached Schooner's Restaurant. Laughing, they shook the ocean spray out of their hair and ducked inside out of the sharp October wind. Once they had a table, they ordered two bowls of New England clam chowder and a bottle of wine.

"Today would have been Harrison's fiftieth birthday," said Shay with a sad smile as they sat down. An unusual statement. Madeline was surprised—this was literally the first time Shay had mentioned Harrison since his death.

Madeline looked at her, "Oh, Shay, I can tell you miss him."

"I do miss him very, very much. I think of Harrison every day. He was the love of my life, and I was his. I will always love him."

Madeline leaned over and kissed Shay on the cheek. "I am so sorry," she said, and there was a soft silence.

After they finished their chowder, Madeline said, "I can't believe you are leaving so soon. It seems like you just got here." She paused and said, "Well, you sort of did just get here," and they looked at each other and smiled.

"I'll call you once you're settled in the UK," said Madeline. "I forgot to ask, where will you be staying?"

"After I'm finished with meetings in London, I'll be staying in one of the golf club's upgraded suites in Sunningdale for the shoot. I've seen preliminary photos, and the suites are big, and gorgeous, the floors are all a pale cherry, the furniture by Chapel Street and the lighting all Italian, mostly Terzani. They are beautiful, drop-dead gorgeous."

"You sound excited."

"I am, plus I've been reading everything I can find on the town of Sunningdale. That famous burglary you mentioned that happened there years ago, the one where the Duchess of Windsor's jewelry was stolen? I've been reading about her. She was a very interesting woman."

"Mrs. Simpson was more than just an interesting American divorcee who married into the British Royal family," said Madeline. "Mrs. Simpson blew it up, big time. She single-handedly changed the line of succession to the throne."

"Yes, I know, that's our Duchess of Windsor all right," said Shay. "Believe it or not, the house where the big burglary happened, Ednam Lodge, is very close to the golf club. I looked at a map, and it's literally next door."

Madeline sighed, "Really, you are that close? Of course, I know the whole story, and I am sick to death of it. I find it hard to believe that after all these years people still get excited about that lost jewelry collection. It isn't lying around somewhere, just waiting to be found. It's long gone. Who knows what really happened to it? Seriously, who cares anymore?"

"There are those who do care," said Shay dismissively, "like me. I bought two books on the duchess in a bookstore in Boston, and they both have pages and pages of four-color photographs of her incredible jewelry. It's funny, but a ruby ring stolen from the duchess reminds me of that ruby ring you have at Coda Gems, except the ruby in the Duchess' ring was a lot bigger, eight carats if you can believe it, and a hundred times more beautiful, no offense. I have totally fallen in love with the Duchess' ring, the head-over-heels kind, and I..."

"Well, don't get too head-over-heels, because that ring of hers is long gone.

I don't know where it is, but it's long gone."

"Maybe but maybe not, nobody really knows. The best part is that I'll be almost on the doorstep of the scene of the crime!"

Madeline sighed, "Shay, it's a waste of time to even think about it."

"Oh, come on, Madeline, it's a fascinating story. It's a real-life mystery."

After Shay paid, they walked back down Nantasket Beach to Madeline's car.

"If you want my professional guess about the jewelry theft," continued Madeline as they drove out of the parking lot, "the duke hid the jewels, claimed there'd been a burglary, had the jewels fenced, and then put in a claim for the insurance money. That is a popular crime with the rich; I've seen it happen before. My point, Shay, is that if there had been a real burglary, at the very least, one or two of the jewelry pieces would have shown up years ago. And then, too, there would have been rumors if the stones had been recut and then sold on the black market. Trust me, people in the jewelry business are all blabbermouths, and word would have leaked out. But that didn't happen. That's another big reason why I do not believe there was a real robbery. I'm positive it was an insurance scam."

"Well, whatever it was, there was a crime, and it was obviously a brilliant one," said Shay, "since law enforcement never solved it. I wonder where 'my' ring is now. I do find the whole thing very curious."

"So now it's 'your' ring?"

"Yes, funny how that happens isn't it? I really would like to know where 'my' ruby ring is."

Madeline had never bothered to wonder what had happened to the jewelry. She could care less about the stupid theft, and it annoyed her that anyone could still be fascinated by the story, especially her own sister.

"In that case," said Madeline, "why don't you just go up and knock on the front door of this Ednam Lodge when you're in Sunningdale and ask if you can just poke around the place, just for a few minutes? Have a look around, you know what I mean? Maybe you could turn up something, like a clue?"

"That's very funny, Madeline. I'd love to, I'd seriously love to. But I won't, since it's owned by an earl or something, and he'd probably call the cops.

From the photos in the books I bought, it's sort of a rambling, old-fashioned place, the perfect scene for a mysterious crime. I really would love to get inside and have a look around. It is just such an incredibly romantic story."

"A burglary is a romantic story?"

"No, but the story of the Duke and Duchess of Windsor certainly is. He gave up everything for love. Everything."

"Well, to be precise," said Madeline, "not quite everything, since even after the theft he was still rich as Croesus. The whole ridiculous story is tedious."

"Well, that's a bit harsh," said Shay. "From what I've read, it was the love affair of the century, maybe even the love affair of the millennium. It's a tragedy that ruby ring he gave her was stolen when she was in Sunningdale."

"Yes, Shay that is all very sad, a true-life heart-wrenching tragedy."

"Well, it is sad," said Shay defensively.

"Somehow," said Madeline, "I am not in the least bit sad."

Shay had to laugh.

* * *

The next day at noon, Madeline and Shay walked into the Troquet restaurant near South Station to meet Felix for lunch.

"It's good to see you again Shay. It's been a while," said Felix when he walked up to their table.

"It has been a long time, Felix. Madeline told me about your promotion. Congratulations are in order."

"Thanks. Tell me, do you still swim with whales?" he said to Shay as he moved his chair closer to Madeline and sat down.

"Very funny. I don't swim with whales," Shay pointed out," because that would be stupid. I photograph them from a distance because I have expensive cameras, but when I need to be close, I stay at least three hundred feet away because the whale could inadvertently kill me. On the other hand, if the whale has a calf, it definitely would kill me, this time on purpose. Either way, I don't ever get too close, just close enough."

"Seems like a dangerous hobby," said Felix.

"Felix, you know I don't photograph whales as a hobby," said Shay, an edge in her voice, "I do it to help save them."

"It's still dangerous," he countered.

"Somebody has to save the whales, and I'm happy to do my part."

"Which is commendable," said Felix quickly.

After they finished their entrees and had coffee, Felix checked his watch and apologized, "I am sorry, but I have to leave for a meeting in Everett." He kissed Shay on the cheek, explaining, "I have become an expert now on liquefied natural gas tankers. I hope your photo shoot in the UK goes well." As he stood up, he said to Madeline, "I'll call you later," and he left.

After the door closed behind him, Madeline and Shay lingered over coffee.

"You are quite cozy with Felix," said Shay, "Well, sort of cozy. You told me he was back in Boston, but I didn't know you were seeing him again."

"'Sort of cozy' is fine with me, and that's the way it will stay," said Madeline as the waiter refilled her coffee cup. "And before you ask, yes, we do talk on the phone, and yes, we do have dinner or lunch from time to time, but that's it. To be clear, I am not now, nor do I ever intend to be in a relationship with Felix again. Divorced couples aren't supposed to have sex. I'm quite sure there's a law against it."

"There isn't," said Shay. "You know what, though, I think he's still in love with you." Madeline abruptly set down her wine glass, and a thin splash dribbled on their table. Shay grabbed a napkin and blotted it up, "The two of you look great together as a couple. In my opinion you and Felix are made for each other, it's like…kismet, which by the way is my new favorite word. I had forgotten that Felix is so good-looking," continued Shay. "He is a handsome man, very handsome."

"Yes, I suppose he is," said Madeline. "I am guessing Felix left to meet with one of his sources for his latest *Spotlight* series. He still spends a lot of time cultivating new sources or staying in touch with his old ones so he's a busy guy. His sources were everything to him when we were married. He did say back then he was sorry for traveling so much, but as I'd told you many times a couple of years ago, I finally just got sick to death of it," she said, her voice flat.

"Madeline, you could have stayed with Felix and…"

"Yes, I could have, but I didn't want to. The problem with 'Happy Ever After' is that it usually comes with a price and in Felix's case, a big one. I decided it wasn't worth it."

She stopped the waiter and ordered a martini, and then reconsidered, calling after him as he walked away, "Make it a double, please, a double martini, straight up, with a twist," and the waiter nodded.

"I always liked Felix," said Shay.

"So did I, and I still do, but being married to him was difficult. If you don't mind, I'd rather not talk about him anymore."

"Fine," said Shay.

There was a lull in the conversation, and Shay sighed, "You know, Madeline, some woman will come along and snap him up. Felix is a catch, and you'll regret…"

"We weren't talking about him anymore, remember?"

"You're right. My memory must be going," said Shay.

"It happens. Speaking of men, are you seeing anyone now?"

Shay shook her head and looked away. "No," she said, twisting the wedding ring on her finger. When she glanced at Madeline, her eyes glistened with tears.

"Never mind," said Madeline. "How about if we leave around 4:00 pm tomorrow for your flight? I know it's early, but you just never know about international delays, so it's better to be safe, etc."

"Sounds great." Shay pulled out her purse and carefully refreshed her pink lipstick, staring at her reflection in her compact before she snapped it shut.

"Do let me know though what Abby thinks of your idea, the…what do you call it…'estate jewelry' one? I think it's a fabulous idea, a good one. All it needs is a little romance, and you'll…"

"We'll just have to see what happens," said Madeline. "I am not sure if Abby will like it, but I hope she will. I am pretty sure it can save Coda Gems."

After Madeline and Shay finished their lunch, the sisters walked outside and parted on the sidewalk, Madeline to go back to the store and Shay to return to Madeline's condo to finish cropping photos for her 'Save the North

Atlantic Right Whale' project.

* * *

Ascot

Frustrated, the Patron sat at the usual table in the Reading Room of the Ascot Library, checking the periodical databases again. Kathleen, the librarian, had abruptly left on vacation to the Shetland Islands three days before, so the fatal 'tragic accident' that had been so carefully set up had to be cancelled at the last minute.

The Patron made a series of brief calls. The new plan had been finalized and would be set in motion the day after Kathleen returned to Ascot from the Shetland Islands.

Another delay was totally unacceptable.

Chapter Two

Boston

When Madeline walked into her kitchen the next morning, Shay was at Madeline's gleaming Wolf stove making breakfast. As Madeline sat down, Shay slid two poached eggs, bacon, and hash browns on a plate and set it in front of her.

"Your timing is perfect, Madeline. I made breakfast for you, just like Mom's," said Shay.

"But better," said Madeline after she dipped a slice of bacon in the egg yolk. "You don't fry the bacon half to death like Mom did. Her bacon had the texture and the taste of greasy cardboard."

"True. But she made it with love."

"Love can be dangerous. We are both lucky we haven't died of congestive heart failure."

"Speaking of love, are you still just a little bit in love with Felix or what?"

"I've told you before, I am most definitely not in love with him. Whatever we had is over, really and truly over. It's forever over. Besides, he just isn't the right one for me, and I don't think that it would…"

The doorbell rang, and Madeline turned and walked out of the kitchen. When she came back a few minutes later, she was carrying a crystal vase with a dozen yellow tulips and a small white card in her hand.

"Thank you, Shay, for sending me these beautiful flowers." Madeline kissed her sister on the cheek and set the vase on the kitchen table beside her plate.

"That was sweet." She looked at Shay, dressed in a pale pink sweater with heavy flounces and a pale pink skirt.

"You look like Little Bo Peep," she said to her sister. "All you need is a shepherd's crook. Seriously though, you're not wearing that for your flight, are you?"

"No, I am not, although personally, I like it because it's pink, even though pink has unfortunately become a favorite color of blowhard, conservative women, and white has been hijacked by the hard-core feminists, so that's out as well. You should talk, though; you dress like a cowgirl. It's mostly your boots," ended Shay.

Madeline laughed, "The cowboy boots are your fault, remember?" She glanced again at Shay's outfit and sighed.

"What are you looking at?" said Shay defensively, "Don't worry, I will change clothes before we leave. For the flight, I'll wear an olive-green dress, something nice and feminine. I need to be ready in case I sit next to 'Mr. Right' on the plane, and we fall in love on the spot. It could happen, you know, it really could."

Madeline shook her head; her sister was an idiot. She pointed to Shay's left hand. "You realize the three-and-a-half-carat diamond ring might be a bit of a problem?"

Shay laughed, "Oh, so now you're giving dating advice?"

"Yes. You should wear the ring around your neck on an 18-kt. chain or something. Now that I think about it, maybe just the diamond."

Shay ignored the comment and said over her shoulder as she walked out of the kitchen to her bedroom, "Just remember, Felix isn't going to wait for you for forever."

"He just might have to," said Madeline as she stacked the breakfast dishes in the sink.

Madeline felt a stab of guilt; she wasn't being fair to Felix. As far as he was concerned, she was already flying too close to the flame. It made no sense for them to see each other anymore. He needed to move on with his life, and so did she.

* * *

Later that afternoon, Madeline dropped Shay off at the terminal for British Airways departures, feeling bad that Shay had left but also, she had to admit, relieved. She had a lot of calls to make.

Madeline went into her study that had been Shay's bedroom, but now that Shay was gone it was just a cold and lonely room. As Madeline folded up the Murphy bed, she found a sheet of paper under the duvet, and the handwriting looked like Shay's, elegant and looping:

"He was from a far-away, foreign land of thin dreams and didn't know how the third act of a fairy tale should end. So, the woman who loved him staged the finale, using an enchanted potion with a handful of silky mane from a unicorn, three discarded dragon's teeth, and an aria from a chunky soprano. The magic potion worked, and the couple lived happily ever after."

At least ten red hearts had been drawn in the margins of the page. Yes, Shay had written this. If Shay was the tattoo type, which she wasn't, she would have had at least four or five heart tattoos somewhere on her body by now.

Madeline wondered who Shay had been writing about, probably not Harrison, since he was from Kansas. Then who was she writing about? Or maybe she wasn't writing about a specific person, she might have just read the paragraph somewhere and liked it.

Shay had been a sweet big sister when Madeline was growing up. Madeline was afraid of spiders when she was seven, and if Shay saw one, she would scoop it up on a piece of paper and drop it outside.

Madeline fell asleep that night worrying about Shay, which woke her up. But ten minutes later, when she fell back to sleep, she was worrying about Coda Gems.

* * *

When Madeline got up the next morning, she had a text from Shay that she'd landed in London and her friend Chip had set up a series of pre-photoshoot meetings with her and his team at the Groucho Club in Soho, an exclusive club for the members of the media and the arts.

Shay's last sentence of her text read, "I can hardly wait to leave for Sunningdale and be next door to the scene of the crime.'" Shay had added three heart emojis as a sign-off, and Madeline sighed.

* * *

At Coda Gems, Madeline had just finished setting up the jewelry displays and was browsing the web checking out estate auctions when Abby walked in the door. After she asked Madeline if Shay's flight to London had left on time, she went to her office. Madeline waited for fifteen minutes to give Abby time to get settled before she walked up to her desk.

"I have a great idea," began Madeline, and after five minutes, she got to the nuts-and-bolts part of how they could turn their store's focus from new jewelry to estate jewelry instead.

"I'll bring in only the best high-end jewelry, of course," said Madeline. "With any luck, we could even include a Patek watch or two. The point is," Madeline ended, "it will make Coda Gems seem less stodgy, not so boringly conventional. To be honest, we are just a 'cookie-cutter' upscale jewelry store, and you know it's true. We aren't all that different from any of the other upscale stores in Boston. My idea is to start with a special section in one of our display cases, called 'Estate Jewelry by Coda Gems', and then we'll expand it. Initially, we'll include about forty estate pieces or more to start. What do you think?"

Abby had been listening intently, but now she frowned. It wasn't that Abby didn't like Madeline's idea. She hated it.

"You seriously want us to sell 'used jewelry'? What you're suggesting would make Coda Gems seem second-rate, or even worse, desperate."

"But Abby, that's not true. We need a competitive edge, and I believe estate jewelry is the key; it can save Coda Gems. This store was my dream, and remember, it was your dream, too."

"In my opinion estate jewelry is a bad idea," insisted Abby. "We have to think about our brand image."

"Not if we bring in high-end estate jewelry pieces. Look, we can't continue to do the same thing over and over. If we don't do something different, we'll go out of business."

"I think your idea would be a total waste of time and effort," said Abby. "We shouldn't change our focus and…"

The two partners argued for ten minutes until Abby threw up her hands and stalked to the back of the store just as Nancy Harhut, one of Madeline's favorite customers, walked in. Nancy was from Connecticut, and as usual, she was dressed in beige, which was *de rigueur* for women from Connecticut, according to Madeline. Five minutes later Nancy bought a $9,000 bracelet, the only bright spot of the day.

Over the next two hours, a thin string of customers came in, three making small purchases, while the rest just walked along their glass cases of jewelry and left.

Madeline and Abby didn't speak to each other until they were getting ready to close the store, when Abby abruptly apologized, "I am sorry Madeline. I was rude, but I am just not convinced estate jewelry is the right move. It's risky. We can talk about this later."

Madeline apologized too, saying she was sorry for telling Abby she was "short-sighted, pretentious, and a snob," but Madeline lied.

She wasn't sorry.

Half an hour late,r the two partners were getting ready to walk out the door when Madeline brought up the estate jewelry idea one more time because she couldn't help it.

"Abby, now that we're speaking again, I really believe we should at least give estate jewelry a try."

Abby's eyebrows furrowed, and after a long minute she sighed, "All right, fine, since you are so convinced, go ahead. You seriously believe you can pull forty estate jewelry pieces together in a decent amount of time? Bear in mind that the pieces must be nothing less than spectacular. For your plan to work, the jewelry pieces must be absolutely, positively spectacular. It will take a lot of effort. Just remember, they must be spectacular. Beautiful is not enough; they must be spectacular."

"Yes, I realize that. Don't worry. I can make it happen. And you don't need to beat the term 'spectacular' to death. I am not hard of hearing."

Abby managed a small smile, but a smile, nonetheless.

Moving into estate jewelry was the only way Madeline could think of to save Coda Gems. She wasn't 100% sure she could track down and sell enough 'spectacular' estate jewelry pieces to make a significant financial difference, but she was pretty sure.

The next morning Madeline emailed her network of gem dealers, asking them to send her photos of 'fabulous and incredible' pieces that were available for consignment. Twenty sent photos of available estate pieces. They were beautiful, yes, but none of them 'spectacular.'

* * *

Felix stopped by Coda Gems the next afternoon on his way out of town for a meeting.

Madeline didn't know how to define her relationship with her ex-husband... if you could call it a relationship. It was certainly an unusual one for ex-spouses, especially without the powerful bond of children. She and Felix talked on the phone about once a week; he called it "catching up," and they had dinner or lunch together from time to time. He was currently very involved in his latest *Spotlight* series investigation into the liquefied natural gas tankers that sailed into Boston Harbor.

"I just had a great idea, let's go out to dinner tonight," said Felix. "You know, we're becoming like an old married couple now," which he must have thought was funny, because he laughed.

She wished he wouldn't make jokes like that. They weren't an old married couple, or even just a plain couple. They were divorced, for God's sake. Besides, Madeline was also nine years older than Felix and she had always been sensitive about the age difference.

"Dinner?" she said with hesitation. "Not tonight. I've got a lot of work to catch up on. I'm working on a new project for the store, which is not going well." She didn't point out to Felix they'd just had lunch a couple of days before.

"Come on, Madeline, don't be so caught up with your career, like you used to, back then, 'in the day'," the phrase he used instead of 'when we were married.' He glanced at her over his reading glasses. "Be spontaneous. Besides, you do have to eat, right?"

"Yes, it's true, I do have to eat, just like other mortals. I guess dinner tonight would be alright."

"Could you possibly be a little more enthusiastic?"

"Let's see, how about, 'I would like nothing better."

"That will do," he said.

They usually only went out to lunch or dinner once or twice a month, so she guessed something must be up.

* * *

They went to Mama Marie's in the North End because, according to Felix, "They have a new chef, a Sicilian guy from Palermo, and *The Globe's* restaurant critic says he is one of the best Italian chefs in the world, so he said I needed to go."

An hour later, they walked into the restaurant, and Madeline said, "Well, we haven't been hit by any stray bullets or caught in the deadly crossfire of a Mafia turf war." She looked around, "so far."

"You didn't waste any time," said Felix, "you went right for the stereotype."

"You are right, Felix, my mistake, that was a stupid comment," she said as a waiter led them to a table, and they ordered drinks. "I usually lean more to the superficial than to the stereotypical."

Felix just looked at her and said with a soft smile, "You forget Madeline, I know your heart."

Shortly after, the waiter came back with Felix's double shot of Glenlivet 18 and Madeline's usual martini, extra dry with a twist, and Felix said, "I've been meaning to ask you how Coda Gems is doing. I saw your ad in *The Globe* last week. I do work there, remember."

"Well, business could be better, a lot better, but we'll see."

"You're not thinking of selling or anything like that, are you?"

"Why, have you heard something?"

"No, but a number of retailers have gone out of business, and I did have to wonder how business was going."

"It is tough right now, but we'll be fine. We need to make some changes. I've been scrambling to locate 'spectacular' pieces of jewelry at a reasonable cost. That is Abby's term, not mine."

He raised his eyebrows but didn't ask her to explain, which was good because she didn't want to talk about jewelry, especially the spectacular kind.

They ordered dinner, and after the waiter left, Felix took a long pull of his scotch. He looked away, and then back at Madeline, staring into her eyes, his gaze steady, unflinching. "Would you like to go away to Mt. Washington this weekend? We went there about seven or eight years ago, remember? I know a lot of the trees will be past their peak foliage now, but not all, and besides, most of the tourists will be gone."

"You realize, of course," said Madeline, "that's quite a long day trip. Round trip, it's at least a seven-hour drive, likely more."

"It is far, so I am thinking we could do an overnight on Saturday at one of the new hotels in North Conway. We could set out early on Saturday morning and come back late Sunday night. What do you think?"

"It would be good to see the White Mountains again," A pause, and she added, casually, "Separate rooms I'm assuming?"

A smile flickered across his face, "Yes, but that's up to you. Remember, I have seen you naked before," he said, "any number of times. I have a photographic memory, but the real thing would, of course, be welcome."

"I think it would be best to go with separate rooms," she said.

"Understood. You can always change your mind, though."

There was an uncomfortable silence. "Felix," she hesitated before she continued, "at the end of our marriage, you were either traveling or working late at *The Globe*. We were basically leading separate lives, and we grew apart. We can't go back to how it used to be."

He looked at her and picked up his scotch, staring at her over the rim for

31

several long moments, his blue eyes gentle. After a long pause, he finally said, "Madeline, I just want to be close to you again. I miss that. A lot."

Which was so honest and unaffected, his longing so unguarded that she could only stare back. He didn't look away. "We were good together," he said.

"Until we weren't."

"I was just too..." and Felix paused.

"'I think the term you are looking for is 'absorbed,'" said Madeline. "You were totally absorbed with your *Spotlight* stories, to the exclusion of everything else, including your wife."

"I was young and callow."

Madeline waved her hand dismissively. "You weren't that young."

Felix laughed, and the moment passed.

With a flourish, the waiter set their entrees on the table: Aubergine Caponata and Pasta con le Sarde. In the silence, they both turned to their entrees.

* * *

After dinner, Felix walked Madeline to her car, illegally parked as usual, but no ticket for once. This time, instead of a kiss on the cheek, he put his arms around her for a long embrace, and then, without looking back, he left for his car in the parking garage. Felix was a man who had his exits down pat.

Once she was home, Madeline lay awake worrying about her estate jewelry project and thinking about Felix until 2:30 am. She wasn't about to sleep with Felix again based on what he wanted. The question was—what did she want? She had missed him after they divorced, and she had forgotten how much until he had come back from Chicago. She remembered the little things, like his slow, sweet smile in the morning when she woke up next to him. When he was there. Yes, she had to admit she still missed him. In a way.

She finally told herself going to New Hampshire with Felix was only one night, after all, and she had nothing to lose. The more she thought about it, the more she liked the idea. There had been times when she had yearned for Felix's lean, hard body next to hers in the middle of the night, and with that thought, she fell asleep.

* * *

She called Felix at six thirty the next morning. She knew he would have already had two cups of coffee, and eggs, sunny side up probably, and three links of sausage. He was a man of habit. But more important, since it was early in the morning, he wouldn't be consumed by his job.

"Thank you for dinner last night," she began, "and about New Hampshire, I would like to go up there with you." She paused and plunged ahead because why not, "Just so you know, I have missed being with you too. And no, we don't need separate rooms."

Madeline could hear the smile in his voice when he said, "I am glad to hear that." She heard Felix take a breath, and then he said, "I have to fly to New York this afternoon for my LNG story, and I'll be in back-to-back meetings tomorrow, so I can't call." It grated on her nerves that he'd brought up his work as an excuse, just like when they'd been married. Then he added, "But let's talk in two days?"

"Fine," she said, "We'll talk."

Madeline spent two hours with a gem dealer in California that afternoon who had seven astonishing Art Deco rings that would be great for her estate jewelry collection. The catch was his consignment price was ridiculously high, so she tried talking him into lowering it. After an hour-long negotiation, the gem dealer abruptly rejected her final offer. Well, he didn't reject her final offer exactly; without a word he had simply hung up.

Madeline hadn't realized how time-consuming lining up estate jewelry pieces would be. What she needed was to find just two or three gem dealers that wanted to sell a big collection of estate jewelry; twenty or thirty pieces each would be great. She'd just have to keep trying. There were gem dealers who sold collections of estate pieces to big jewelers like Saks Fifth Avenue, but she learned their consignment rates were close to regular retail, so the profit margin was slim to none, and working with them was not worth it. She had no choice but to put together an estate jewelry collection the hard way, piece by piece. Which might take a very long time.

Chapter Three

London

Special Agent Basil Talbot of the British intelligence agency MI5 warily waited in the lobby of their headquarters on the Thames for Hannah Davis, their recent ex-director General, to walk through the front door.

Basil, in his mid-twenties, had met Hannah twice in his less than twelve-month MI5 career. However, he was aware that in her controversial seventeen years at the helm of the agency, there were those who regarded her as a legend in the intelligence world. Then there were those who thought it was about time the woman was dead, the kind of people who didn't like to wait around for natural causes.

And here he was, about to temporarily work for her.

The front door swung open, and Basil looked up as Hannah walked in. She was striking rather than beautiful, with the classic air of an opera diva, imperious and aware of her celebrity, elegant too, but with an edge. Hannah was tall, her dark hair dramatically streaked with gray and pulled back with ebony combs.

Basil knew it was rumored that Hannah used a stiletto with an eighteen-kt gold handle as a letter opener, which he dismissed as an exaggeration, but that was before he met her. As he went up to her he couldn't look away from her hazel eyes flecked with gold and red.

His six-week assignment was to be Hannah's glorified dogsbody, tying up any loose ends for her, a position he had volunteered for. Basil ran his fingers through his long red hair and nervously adjusted his tie. He hoped he hadn't made a big mistake.

As Director General at MI5, Hannah had been responsible for identifying domestic threats within the UK, which meant that she had worked in the country's shadows for years, collecting and analyzing the secrets of UK citizens and its shifty-eyed visitors. Hannah's father and her grandfather had both held the Director General position at the agency, and as a result Hannah knew, going back for over sixty years, where all the bodies were buried.

Basil smiled when he reached Hannah, and they shook hands, and he led her to the elevator and up to his office on the fifth floor, his diploma from Oxford's business school hanging in pride of place above his walnut desk. He waved Hannah to one of the worn brown chairs across from his desk, and she glanced around and then sat, her eyes fixed on his. She rarely blinked, a habit of hers he had found unnerving during his short briefing with her the week before.

Basil moved a stack of folders on his desk to the side. He would have preferred to deal with Hannah by phone, but she had insisted on coming to his office.

"I'm glad we'll be working together, even if just for a short time," she said.

His short assignment with Hannah was to wrap up any unfinished business for her after her sudden retirement. Finalizing her pension was easy, just a matter of overseeing dull agency paperwork, but he was also to follow up on an old and unsolved crime for her. He had been told in his briefing that Hannah was preoccupied with an old, mysterious burglary that happened years ago in Sunningdale. Years before, the crime had made headlines around the world, a brazen burglary that Scotland Yard, in charge of the investigation, never had solved, even after they brought in MI5.

A thief had stolen high-end jewelry in October of 1946 and the jewelry had simply vanished, with the thief never identified, much less arrested and charged.

Hannah pulled a thick file folder from her calf-skin attaché case and handed it to him. "As you are probably aware, the theft of jewelry from the Duchess of Windsor happened on my father's watch when he was Director General," she said. "However, it was unfortunate the theft was never solved, which troubled my father up to the very day he died," she paused, "as if that had been a failing on his part, which, of course, is ridiculous." She looked up, "I assume you know my father, Gregory Davis, was the youngest ever Director General of MI5?"

Basil didn't know that, but he nodded anyway.

"Nevertheless, the honor of MI5 is at stake here, which is important to me. I have spent my entire professional life at this agency, and my record, as well as my family's record, is one of extraordinary service and dedication to the UK. It's up to me to protect that legacy," said Hannah, and she smiled briefly, "That's why, Basil, I need your help."

Basil opened the folder, glanced at the stack of papers inside, and set the file on his desk. He looked at her, waiting.

Hannah continued, "The problem is even now, from time to time, there are ridiculous stories about that old burglary that continue to crop up, and I want you to check them out and let me know what has been said or written. Although I have officially left the agency, I want all those old stories permanently quashed. As you know, my family has overseen MI5 for three generations," she said, "and I am proud of our service to the UK. I don't want that heritage tarnished, especially now that I have retired."

She pointed to the file, "I want you to let me know if someone, anyone, is poking around Sunningdale, looking for old clues to this case. Why? Because if not properly handled, the whole thing could blow up into a ridiculous media frenzy." She stared at Basil, her eyes glittering. "There is nothing," she continued, "that I dislike more than amateur sleuths, who are just busybodies. The Davis family legacy is at stake here, and I want to know if anything, anything about that burglary, comes up again. Anywhere. That is where you come in. I need to know who is still interested and why. And I need to know it now while I still have a bit of clout left at MI5."

Basil nodded in acknowledgment, thankful that at least she hadn't asked to be put up for an OBE.

So far.

Basil slid the file from Hannah next to his battered briefcase. He'd go over it that night and see if there had been anything new on the case, but he doubted it. The old burglary hadn't been actively worked for decades.

They talked for another thirty minutes about Scotland Yard's investigation into the crime in the 1940s, which to him seemed lackluster despite the available manpower, but he wasn't about to mention that, and then, finally, Hannah left.

* * *

When Basil's cell phone rang on his desk at MI5 at 9:00 am two days later he glanced at the caller ID and sighed. He answered immediately.

"Do you have anything for me about Sunningdale?" began Hannah. "I thought you would have been in touch by now."

Basil stared at the phone. He'd had the file from Hannah for exactly two and a half days, and he sighed. The woman was too much. He had done some preliminary checking with local authorities, and that was it. The good news was there hadn't been reports of anyone poking around searching for information on the old theft, which, yes, had been a famous crime once, a long time ago.

"If there was anything, I'd have let you know immediately," said Basil. "There has been nothing, absolutely nothing, that has come up so far. I did speak with my contacts at the Royal Borough of Windsor and Maidenhead— that's the council for Sunningdale," he added unnecessarily. "And I also spoke to the local police, in Sunningdale and in Ascot too. They all told me that the old burglary hadn't shown up on anyone's radar. I left my cellphone number with them in case anyone walks in the door with questions. I also left a message for Jonah Musgrave, the owner of the Sunningdale Golf Club, as well as one with the Earl of Dudley, the owner of Ednam Lodge, and scene of the crime, but he is in Croatia for two months. I'll follow up if I don't hear back from either of them. In addition, as I'd mentioned, I'll continue to monitor the local newspapers."

He glanced at Hannah's thick file on the theft still on his desk. Its most sensational aspect was that the victim of the crime was a duchess, the wife of the Duke of Windsor, the man who, from Jan. 20, 1936–Dec. 10, 1936, had been King Edward VIII of the United Kingdom and the Dominions of the British Empire, as well as the Emperor of India. He had been one of the most powerful men on earth, but the king-emperor had walked away from his titles, power, and vast estates for Mrs. Simpson, a twice-divorced American. A decision that was termed by journalist H.L. Mencken at the time as "The Biggest News Story since the Resurrection."

"I need to make sure that you're on top of the situation," said Hannah. "I have to be confident that you will be observant, as well as proactive." Her tone was textbook law enforcement, brusque and to the point.

"Of course, and…" began Basil.

"Just to be clear, I am trusting that you will be thorough. Very thorough. Do let me know when you hear back from your contacts or pick up any… untoward interest in the burglary."

Basil shifted uncomfortably in his chair. He was up for a promotion as supervisor of a digital intelligence team, the reason he had volunteered for the short-term assignment with the Ex-Director General. A good review from Hannah could help him clinch that promotion. But now he realized a bad review from her could not just jeopardize his rise through the ranks of the agency. It could get him fired.

Hannah continued, "It is ridiculous that years ago, a burglar apparently climbed up a drainpipe on an outside wall of the earl's home to the second floor, then slipped into the duke and duchess' bedroom through an outside window while the servants were having tea downstairs, and grabbed a titanium case of her jewelry that…

"That is now worth over twenty million dollars," interrupted Basil.

Hannah ignored his comment and continued, "After the duke and duchess left for dinner in London that day, two Scotland Yard bodyguards remained on duty in the earl's kitchen. What were they doing while the jewelry was stolen, rummaging through the cupboards looking for a biscuit?

"Basil, your first responsibility will be to work in the background, slow and steady, but most important, not spark any new interest in the old crime, which is just a waste of time."

There was a silence, and he said, "Why do you think anyone would be interested after all these years?"

There was a long pause before Hannah said, "If I had that kind of information, I wouldn't have needed you to check into it now, would I?" she said sharply and disconnected.

He tapped his fingers nervously on his walnut desk; that conversation had not exactly gone well. Basil was in an impossible situation. He was now on the hook for an ending to an old, unsolved crime, working for a powerful woman who thought he was an idiot.

* * *

The next morning Hannah invited Basil for lunch near his office, which he took as a good sign after the difficult ending to their phone call the day before.

"I thought it would be helpful," she had said on the phone, "if we got together outside the office. I apologize this is so last-minute, but are you available to for lunch today at noon?"

"Yes, no problem, I can meet at noon."

"Thank you. How about the Blue Cardinal at 100 Bridge St.?

"Perfect. I look forward to it," said Basil.

When Basil arrived at the restaurant Hannah was sitting at a table by a high arched window, staring out at the snarled traffic below. As he walked up, he saw her check her gold Rolex when she spotted him, and she smiled. She stood when the maitre'd led him to her table. Basil was glad he was two minutes early.

"I appreciate your meeting me on such short notice," said Hannah, her thick dark hair pulled back in a chignon, "and I appreciate your being on time."

He knew Hannah was married, but he noticed she didn't wear a wedding ring, not even a simple gold band. Basil did have to wonder what her husband was like; formidable too, no doubt.

After they ordered, Hannah took a leather folder out of her briefcase and showed him a photo of a hard-eyed man in an olive military jacket, with curling brown hair, staring straight into the camera, his posture ramrod straight. "That's my father," she said, "Gregory Davis."

Hannah set the leather folder back in her briefcase. "Both he and my grandfather were famous, not just within MI5, but in the international intelligence world."

Basil had already studied the list of domestic attacks that Hannah and her family had foiled over the last nearly sixty years. The press has labeled the Davis family "a Spy Dynasty" by the press, a label he was sure MI5 did not appreciate. Regardless, the Davis family had a very impressive record of domestic terror arrests and convictions, but Hannah's reputation had come to overshadow even her father's. Her success rate in tracking down and convicting domestic terrorists had been extraordinary.

An hour later, Basil wasn't quite sure why Hannah had invited him for lunch since most of her conversation over lunch had been about her father. After a waiter took away their plates and they sat over tea, she still had not mentioned a word about the stolen jewelry. That was what this meeting was about, wasn't it?

Basil brought the conversation back to the theft, "I think the Duchess's jewelry theft was a fascinating crime," he said as he poured cream into his third cup of tea.

Hannah smiled, "Yes, it is an interesting one, isn't it? But I do wish people would stop with the speculation. My father talked for years about how frustrated he was that he couldn't solve the crime when he was the head of MI5. He always said that it should have been easy, but obviously, it wasn't. People should just leave it alone, for God's sake. It's over. It's in the past.

"Basil, I want you to alert me immediately if anyone is running around, asking ridiculous questions," said Hannah. "The anniversary of the theft is coming up, which never fails to push the damn amateur sleuths into overdrive. They can't seem to resist coming up with new theories, or even resurrecting old ones. Personally, I'd like to have them all arrested and thrown in prison, which unfortunately is not possible these days."

Basil wasn't sure if he should agree with her, so he didn't.

"I do appreciate your working with me Basil," she said, "so just let me know if there is anything you need."

He smiled, "What do you think happened to her jewelry?"

Her tone was sharp, "Why do you want to know?"

"It's certainly relevant, isn't it, to stopping the rumors?" he said, surprised.

"There are those, and personally I think they are correct, who believe the jewelry was smuggled out of the UK immediately after the theft."

"Out of the country?" said Basil.

Hannah looked at him, "Yes, that's what I just said."

He stared at her and then looked away.

"Every now and then," she began casually changing the subject, "while we're working together, I may well ask you for your assistance with issues that might come up, nothing major of course, just little things that I'll need you to follow up on for me. I know I can trust you."

'Bingo,' Basil thought to himself. This was the real reason for the lunch.

"Of course," he said, and he knew what he should say next, so he did, "Just let me know what I can do."

They left the restaurant ten minutes later and parted on the sidewalk.

When Basil got back to the office, he flipped through the local newspapers delivered to his desk every day now, looking for any mention of the old burglary, but there was nothing.

Hannah was smart, very smart, and Basil was relieved she still considered him part of her team. She was well known in the agency for solving important and intractable cold cases, the kind that made headlines.

How could he help her with the burglary case? It made sense for him to closely follow the aspects of the case and figure out what he could do for her.

The thought made Basil feel good. His mission was an honorable one.

* * *

The next morning, when Basil walked in his MI5 office at Thames House he had seven voicemails on his desk phone. The first one was from Hannah, who as usual launched into her message, a thank you for meeting her for lunch, and then a click as she hung up.

Basil saved her message with a flick of his finger and worked his way through the others.

The fifth message was from Luella Kloberdanz, a reporter with *The Times.* He knew her from the weekly press conferences he'd attended a couple of years ago at Ten Downing Street when she was writing *ad nauseum* about Brexit for *The Times.* He remembered her as a whip-smart brunette with sparkling, dark brown eyes. He listened to her message again. He'd forgotten how determined she could be.

"Hello Basil, this is Luella Kloberdanz. We met about six or seven times at the Ten Downing Street press conferences, the Brexit ones. Since then, I've moved from financial reporting for the paper to feature writing, and I'm looking for a bit of background information on a story that Christopher, my damn editor, wants right away, and I thought you might be able to help since you're with MI5. It's one of those 'unsolved crime stories' that my editor loves. So please call me as soon as you can. And no, it's not Jack the Ripper, thank God, but it's almost as bad. It's that jewelry robbery, the Duchess of Windsor one, God rest her soul. Do please call me, today if possible. I would really appreciate talking to you."

Luella rattled off a number and disconnected.

Basil wrote down her number, then drew a line through it and dropped it in his Out Box. He wasn't about to answer any of her questions, first and most importantly because it was totally against MI5 policy for him to give out any information, and second, Hannah would have heart failure if she knew he had talked to a reporter, so he wouldn't mention it. She would likely write a 'fluff piece' article anyway because there was nothing new to write about, so no need to bother Hannah with it.

He sent Luella a brush-off text, "Nice to hear from you, but I'm on Special Assignment now. Scotland Yard's press office should be able to help you out with any questions you have. Good luck with your story!" and he left it at that.

Regardless, he continued to pay attention to the local news. It was good the anniversary of the crime was coming up, because the anniversary of the crime would likely be mentioned soon in the media. Something was bound to come up.

Basil had been told that none of the Duchess' jewelry pieces stolen that day had ever surfaced, except for a pearl necklace the thief had apparently dropped when he ran away from the scene of the crime that afternoon. Or, and Basil stopped, maybe that was part of a plan to throw investigators off the scent, to make the burglary seem amateurish and last minute, and not a crime committed by professionals?

The key question, though, was what had happened to the jewelry. Not a single piece of the stolen jewelry, outside of the dropped pearl necklace, had ever shown up anywhere in the world. The entire jewelry collection, the stones as well as the platinum and 18 kt gold settings, had simply vanished, which was unusual in any jewelry theft.

Basil was aware what that could mean; the collection could still be intact, hidden away somewhere by an unknown person, who after eighty years was undoubtedly by dead now. So where had the thief hidden the jewelry? Basil went through the MI5 file from Hannah one more time looking for any mention of hidden jewelry, but he didn't find anything.

* * *

That afternoon, Basil called the Earl of Dudley again, the ninth earl if he had his genealogy right, whose rambling estate in Sunningdale had been the sixth Earl of Dudley's second home in the 1940s and the unfortunate crime scene of the famous jewelry theft. However, he only got as far as the man's officious butler, who told him, "His lordship is still out of the country, and it is not known when he will return."

Basil had also been able to speak briefly to Jonah Musgrave, owner of the Sunningdale Golf Club, who told him, "No one has asked about the burglary for at least twenty years. I have no information for you," and Jonah hung up.

By the end of the day, Basil had no information about anyone looking for information on the theft, except, of course, for Luella, who was just a 'fluff-piece' features writer now, and she didn't matter, so he didn't mention her to Hannah.

* * *

Ascot

Shortly after 9:00 am the next morning a text message abruptly appeared on the Patron's cellphone screen.

"The subject landed at Heathrow from the Shetland Islands late last night and left for work at 8:55 am this morning. You can expect results within twenty-four to forty-eight hours."

The Patron gave a satisfied smile and sent a one-word reply, "Acknowledged."

Five minutes later, the Patron left the office and went outside to the waiting car.

Chapter Four

Sunningdale

Shay called Madeline at 7:00 am Boston time. "I thought I'd let you know that I am in Sunningdale now, in my big luxury suite at the clubhouse, and it is breathtaking! It has a huge fireplace, enormous windows, and even a small stainless-steel kitchen.

"I had all my cameras and lenses equipment shipped to the UK before I left San Francisco, so I'm ready to begin. I can start shooting three of the guest rooms in a day or so after I get my cameras set up."

"That's great. What do you think of Sunningdale?" said Madeline.

"It's hard not to love this town; it's upscale and gorgeous, a village, really. Chip gave me a tour, and I had him drive past Ednam Lodge, that's where that Duchess of Windsor burglary happened. It's a sprawling, old-fashioned place, and he said I can walk there from there from my suite in less than ten minutes if I go down a private access road. I'll take a couple of pictures for you. This afternoon, I'm going to the library over in Ascot, right next to Sunningdale, and read up on the stolen jewelry this afternoon. I'm sure they'll have at least eight or ten books on the Duchess, and no doubt the librarian there will help me with other sources."

"Shay, aren't you going a little overboard on this?"

"I can't help it," laughed Shay, "I am literally next door to the scene of The Crime of the Last Century. Lucky me."

"If you consider that lucky," laughed Madeline. "Before I forget, can you give me Chip's phone number just in case I can't reach you?"

Madeline wrote down the number Shay gave her and put it in her phone. The sisters said goodbye and disconnected.

* * *

London

Later that afternoon, Basil's cell phone buzzed with a text. Tisha Lloyd, the SVP of Domestic Surveillance at MI5, wanted to see him in her office for a few minutes "when it is convenient."

Basil immediately left for her office, and when she saw him standing in her doorway, she motioned him to come in. He glanced at her framed map of the British Empire circa 1935 behind her desk. Tisha had an old-fashioned, idealistic view of empires.

Tisha was, as usual, dressed like a Sloan Ranger; Loro Piana knitwear, a Hermes scarf, and a string of pearls. Her black, braided hair fell down her back, and the stack of gold bracelets on her right wrist gleamed against her caramel skin. Her most striking feature however was her wideset eyes, almond-shaped and a pale brown. Basil had looked up her application to MI5; Tisha had listed the color of her eyes as 'perceptive.'

Tisha had been Basil's mentor when he'd first joined the agency, and she had taken him under her wing. She thought he was smart and dedicated, but very naive. The naive part had troubled her and still did. Tisha watched him carefully.

"I hope all is well with you?" she said as he sat across from her.

Basil noticed the thank you gift he'd given her ten months before on her desk, an expensive ebony and silver replica of Sherlock Holmes' magnifying glass, except this one was forty-power.

"I understand that you're working on a short-term project with Hannah," she said, "and I thought I'd check in with you and see how that is going since you are my favorite Covert Operations Specialist named Basil."

"I am glad for the opportunity to work with Hannah," said Basil. "I am learning a lot. She can be very intense, but I'm sure you know that."

Tisha laughed, "I do. She has, or rather, she had a demanding job. Has she mentioned her father, Gregory Davis?"

"Yes, she has mentioned him a number of times," he said, his tone deadpan, and they both smiled.

"I worked for Hannah in cybersecurity years ago," said Tisha. "She was very kind to me, and I know that even after people who worked for her left MI5, they told me she was good about staying in touch with them, birthdays, holidays, etc. I guess she was just like her father Gregory; he stayed in touch with former employees as well." Tisha settled back in her chair, "I just want to make sure that she is not making your life too difficult wrapping up her unfinished business."

"Hannah does have her obsessions," Basil said.

Tisha sighed, "That is one way to put it. She always has been passionate about her job. She was very effective as Director General, but Basil, just be careful, be cautious."

"Are you warning me?" he asked, surprised.

Tisha stood up from behind her desk and went to the door, made sure it was closed tight, and went back to her desk.

"This conversation between us is, of course, confidential," she said. "I have heard rumors about former MI5 employees working for Hannah. Do you know anything about that?"

Basil shook his head no and said, "I am not sure I know what you are talking about. Do you mean consulting?"

"I see," she said. "Yes, I suppose you could call it that," and she paused before continuing, "I joined a team here two months ago that has been 'monitoring' a number of former employees who have 'consulted' with Hannah. In case you didn't know, 'consulting' isn't unusual in the intelligence world. However, the team is investigating allegations of blackmail and bribery and, potentially worse, by MI5. Nothing definite, but something may have been going on for a long time, a very long time, for years. Still, they are allegations only, and I hope they are not true. Have you heard anything about that? This is all highly confidential, of course."

"No, I haven't heard rumors about anyone working as a consultant for Hannah after they left MI5. I haven't heard anything at all."

He looked at Tisha, waiting for her to say more. However, she hesitated and then changed the subject.

"Were you aware Hannah is writing a book? Although by now, she may have already finished it. She told me about her book over a year ago. It's mostly about her father's history with MI5, and of course, it includes her career as well. She mentioned me a couple of times in her book, and I was flattered."

"I didn't think agents in intelligence agencies were allowed to write books," said Basil.

"She is retired and is no longer an employee, so Hannah can do and say whatever she wants, so long as top-secret information isn't made public. That is probably why she took an early retirement from MI5."

"I wondered why she retired so abruptly."

"I can get you reassigned," said Tisha. "It might not be a bad idea."

"No thanks, I'm fine. To be honest, I like working with Hannah on that old, unsolved burglary case. I can learn a lot."

"Basil, let me know if anything comes up with Hannah that you...well, anything that you think I might like to know about. Things that just seem, let's say, off-kilter."

"Of course," said Basil. This was weird he thought, spies spying on spies.

Tisha's phone rang, and after she glanced at the caller ID. "Sorry, Basil, I need to take this, but do let me know if you come across anything that strikes you as unusual. Call me day or night. I'm serious. I want to know how things are going with you, so stay in touch."

They shook hands, and he left Tisha's office. It sounded to him like Hannah might be in some sort of trouble at MI5, and he was anxious to come up with something he could do to help her. Hannah was rarely in London; she and her husband lived somewhere in Berkshire.

It might be helpful if he could listen in on her phone conversations. Even though she was no longer with MI5 she still switched burner cell phones multiple times a day, 'out of habit' she had joked to Basil the day before. Basil decided that he'd try and keep track of them anyway just in case he got lucky with scanning. He was a Covert Operations Specialist after all.

⁕ ⁕ ⁕

Sunningdale

Shay called Madeline from Sunningdale when she was in heavy traffic on the Central Artery on her way to an early lunch with a gem dealer, so she let call go to voicemail. Shay's message was short, "Call me?"

Madeline called ten minutes later, and Shay answered on the first ring.

"I need to tell you that I haven't been able to stop thinking about the jewelry robbery," began Shay. "It is such a fascinating story, and here I am, right where it happened! I've been talking to people in Sunningdale and in Ascot, too, that's the town next to it, and I just finished reading another book about the Duchess of Windsor. Somebody must know what happened the night of the burglary. Somebody, somewhere knows where her jewelry is, I just need to dig a little deeper."

"What do you mean, 'dig a little deeper'?" said Madeline suspiciously.

"Well, the crime is fascinating, but it doesn't make sense, so a couple of hours ago, I went to the library in Ascot and talked to Kathleen, the head librarian there. She's smart, shrewd, and very helpful. She knew exactly what newspaper and magazine articles I should read. Kathleen even gave me a list.

"Yesterday I drew a map of Sunningdale and the local landmarks, like Holy Trinity, a big, Gothic church here, and of course the Sunningdale Golf Club. I know the thief ran across the greens of the golf course after the burglary, but I don't know where he went after that. He could have gone in any direction." Shay laughed, "What I need to find is a clue, or something."

"Don't be ridiculous, the trail is very cold now, as in ice-cold after all these years. Thousands of people have walked across the golf course since then, and I do mean thousands."

"I know the trail is cold," she said, "but there must be a couple of clues somewhere to indicate what really happened. Somebody missed something, either the local cops or Scotland Yard, or whoever, somebody missed something. Since I'm here after all, I may as well check into it, and maybe I'll find 'my' ruby ring."

"That's crazy," said Madeline.

"One never knows. The good news is that I'm off on a big adventure this afternoon in twenty minutes with Kathleen, my new best friend. I met her this morning at the big library in Ascot. She's going to pick me up and we're going out to dinner in an hour. She said she has a 'blockbuster' thought about what was really behind the theft, which I'm dying to hear. You know, Madeline, this whole story is just like a thrilling adventure movie. I do love being 'on the trail' of a fascinating crime in pokey little Sunningdale."

"You are crazy to be so wrapped up in this ridiculous and 'supposed' burglary," said Madeline. "I told you I'm pretty sure it was only an insurance fraud scam, so just let it go."

"I can't," said Shay, "After all, you're the one who told me to take photos of that house where the burglary happened," she said with a laugh. "You're pretty bossy for a baby sister and—"

"Younger sister," interjected Madeline.

"Sorry," said Shay abruptly, "but I have to go; Kathleen will be here any minute. I'll let you know tomorrow if I find out anything interesting tonight at dinner," and Shay hung up.

* * *

Boston

At the store, Madeline spent an hour working on her estate jewelry idea, trying to negotiate the consignment of an invisibly set emerald ring and a matching bracelet and exquisite necklace she knew Abby would love, but in the end, the gem dealer, after forty minutes, of refusing to budge on his exorbitant price. She suggested he think about it, and she'd call him the next day. The gem dealer told her his price was final and not to bother calling him back.

She realized her great, fabulous idea was a lot harder than she thought it would be. The only thing she could do was try harder. Finding available estate jewelry pieces wasn't difficult, but finding ones that were 'spectacular,' Abby's big stipulation, was making her search very difficult.

An hour later, she struck gold and was able to secure a 24 kt gold mesh Harry Winston bracelet at a decent consignment rate after a difficult conversation. It was a ray of real hope, at last, a slim one, but she was getting somewhere, sort of.

After dinner, Madeline watched a movie on TV, and as she got ready for bed, she thought about Felix and wished she hadn't said she'd go with him to New Hampshire. She couldn't see how it could possibly end well. What had she been thinking? Besides, she needed to work on her estate jewelry collection.

She went to bed and fell asleep almost immediately.

Four hours later she was woken out of a dead sleep by the shrill ring of her cell phone. She peered at the long phone number on caller ID and hesitantly answered, "Hello?"

A man with a British accent asked, "Is this Madeline Lane?"

"Who are you, and why are you calling in the middle of the night?"

"Sorry to wake you. I am calling from the UK. My name is Dr. Ben Grimm, and I am an A&E doctor at Heatherwood Hospital in Ascot; in the States, I would be called an ER doctor. You are listed on Mrs. Shay Wolf's passport as her sister, and you are her emergency contact. Is that correct?"

"Yes, she is my sister. What has…"

"Your sister Shay Wolf was in an automobile accident, a bad one, a very bad one a couple of hours ago in Ascot. She has a concussion and several bad contusions, but her injuries are not life-threatening."

"Oh my God," said Madeline, and sat up in bed, wide awake now, her grip tightening on her phone. "I thought she was in Sunningdale. Where is

Ascot?"

Chapter Five

Boston

"Ascot is a small town next to Sunningdale," said Dr. Grimm to Madeline, "and both are not that far from London. Mrs. Wolf is in stable condition, and she is now in our ICU, where her concussion is being monitored. She will remain in the ICU for observation, but let me repeat, she is in stable condition. Your name and phone number are listed in her US passport as her primary contact, so that's why I am calling you."

Madeline flicked on the bedside lamp, "But she's alright? You said she's alright? What happened?"

At that moment, Madeline couldn't avoid a stab of guilt. After all, she had insisted Shay go to the UK for the photo shoot.

"Your sister sustained a concussion, but she was conscious when she was brought into the A&E, which is good. No bones were broken, but she did sustain significant bruising on her chest, face, and arms. I ordered a CAT scan of her chest, and there were no punctures to her lungs, and another scan did not show any abnormalities of blood vessels. However, she is confused, and her speech is affected, which is normal with a concussion, but again, her condition is stable. I've ordered an MRI for first thing tomorrow.

"Mrs. Wolf was a passenger in a car that was hit broadside by a tow truck," continued the doctor. "The driver of the tow truck drove away immediately after the accident, and the truck was found an hour ago, abandoned five miles away. We don't know who the driver was, or where he, or she is now, but the tow truck had been reported as stolen."

"Can I talk to Shay now?"

"No. She has been sedated and is sleeping, but you can talk to her in a couple of hours. A preliminary CT scan did show swelling of her brain, but we'll know more after the MRI."

"When Shay wakes up," said Madeline, "can you please have someone let her know that you've been in touch with me and I will be at the hospital as soon as I can? It's 4:00 am in Boston, but I will book the first flight I can get to London right now. Is the number you called me from the number for the hospital?"

He gave Madeline another phone number, as well as the address of the Heatherwood hospital, which she scrawled on a pad of paper on her bedside stand.

"You will have someone call me immediately if there are any changes in her condition? If I don't answer, they should just leave a message," asked Madeline, "since I will be on a plane soon."

"Yes, of course."

"You said Shay was a passenger. What about the driver of the car?"

"Unfortunately, the female driver was declared dead at the scene of the accident. I can't release her name until her family has been notified."

Madeline's heart stopped, and she said, "How horrible, how very tragic. Thank you for getting in touch with me and for looking after my sister."

"I will let her know we spoke. I am sorry to give you such shocking news, but again, your sister is in stable condition. Unfortunately, I need to be in emergency surgery shortly, so goodbye," and he hung up.

Madeline threw the covers off the bed and jumped out of bed.

* * *

Forty-five minutes later, Madeline had a ticket to London, had taken a shower, packed a suitcase, stowed her laptop in her bulging carry-on, and was in an Uber on her way to Logan Airport. She called Abby from the Uber and told her about the accident, but that Shay was in stable condition and that she was flying to London in a couple of hours.

"Oh my God, how awful," said Abby. "Poor Shay, how terrible. Please tell her I am thinking of her."

"I'm not sure when I'll be back in Boston. I won't return until I can bring Shay with me, which shouldn't be more than a couple of days or so, but it might be more and…"

"Madeline, don't worry about that now."

"Thanks. I am thinking that Martin could fill in for me at the store until I get back."

"I'm sure he will. I'll call him in a couple of hours."

Martin was a retired jeweler who ran Coda Gems on Saturdays and Sundays, since Madeline and Abby took the weekends off, or rather used to. To save money she and Abby now took turns running the store on the weekends. Martin was smart, funny, and efficient. However, it did bother Madeline that when the rich of Boston walked in their door, he all but gave a deep bow. He called it showing respect, but Madeline called it something else.

Madeline then called Shay's friend Chip. "I am Madeline, Shay Wolfe's sister, calling from Boston. I wanted you to know I received a call from the Heatherwood Hospital in the UK," and she glanced down at her notes, "in Ascot. Shay was in a car accident there several hours ago. I am at the airport now, and my flight to London leaves in three hours, and I will be going directly to the hospital. She has a concussion, but she is in stable condition. No broken bones or anything."

"What? Oh my God! I just talked to her a couple of hours ago. I can't believe it, how awful for her…she was so excited to be here, and I was so happy to be working with her again. I do love her you know. But she's alright? What happened?"

She told Chip what little she knew about Shay's condition and the accident.

"We were supposed to have a late breakfast this morning," said Chip, "and I would have been frantic if she didn't show up and I couldn't get ahold of her. I'll let the team at the club know. Obviously, the photo shoot will have to be rescheduled."

"I'll call you after I see her in the hospital," said Madeline. "I know Shay was looking forward to working with you. She said you are a genius."

"She is too kind; please give her my regards. Tell her I'll come to the hospital later this afternoon to see her, and she's not to worry about anything. And Madeline, I don't want you to stay in a hotel. After you see Shay, you can stay in her suite here, at the golf club. It's not that far from the hospital in Ascot, and it will just be easier for you, and it will make me feel better. Do you have the address for the club? If not, I'll text it to you. By the way, have you ever driven in the UK?"

"No, never."

"Well, don't rent a car. I'll have the club send a car for you." Chip gave her a phone number and told her to call when she was ready to leave the hospital. "With a little bit of notice," said Chip, "I can arrange to have a car and driver take you back and forth to see Shay while she is in the hospital."

"That is very kind of you, incredibly kind, thank you. I will appreciate a place to stay after I see Shay, as well transportation. I'll pay you for these expenses before I leave the UK, because…"

"Madeline, don't worry about it. Shay came here to work for the club, so it's up to us to look after her while she's in the hospital, and to look after you too. I insist. We are glad to do it, and I know that Jonah, the owner of the golf club, would agree."

Madeline heard voices in the background again, and then Chip said, "I need to go, but I will have everything set up for you at the club's office by the time you land at Heathrow, and they will be expecting you. Have a good flight. I need to prepare for a big presentation tomorrow, so I have to go, but tell Shay we are thinking about her. All I can say is, thank God it looks like she's going to be alright," and Chip disconnected.

Madeline could only hope that was true.

* * *

Madeline checked her watch; she had an hour before she could board her plane to London. She walked over to a Starbucks, ordered a Venti hot coffee, and went to her gate. It was now 5:25 am in Boston, and Felix would have already showered and had at least one, possibly two cups of coffee to jump-start his day. She called him.

"It's me. I'm at Logan Airport," she said when he picked up, "Shay has been in a car accident in the UK and I'm at Logan, waiting to board a plane to London in an hour. She is..."

"Good God, in an accident? How is she? Is she okay?

"She has a concussion and is bruised, but no broken bones or, so it seems, nothing life-threatening. I'll let you know more once I see her. The accident happened in a town outside London. I'm not sure how long I'll be gone. It could be a couple of days or maybe a week. I'll be in touch," she ended.

"Madeline, I am so sorry this has happened, and thank you for letting me know. How are you doing?"

"Me? I'm fine, but worried, and nervous of course. Hold on for just a second," and then she came back on the line. "Sorry, but I have to go, there's an announcement about my flight."

"Of course. And Madeline, do take care, alright?"

"I will."

"I was looking forward to spending this weekend with you," he said. "Let me know how Shay is doing." After a pause, he added, "Goodbye, my love," and they both disconnected.

Madeline stared at the phone. When they were first married that's what he used to say at the end of their calls, the time when they were in love. She went up to the check-in desk, but the announcement was just about a twenty-minute boarding delay, so she stuck her phone in her pocket and checked her watch again. For the next twenty minutes she watched bleary-eyed travelers walking down the long corridor to their gates through her own bleary eyes.

* * *

Flight to the UK

Once she was on the plane and settled into her seat, she gave a pleasant but not too friendly smile to the stout man next to her. Shortly after, the jet lumbered down the runway and pushed its heavy body into the overcast sky. Madeline was restless. She had forgotten to buy a book at the airport to read on the flight.

Madeline fell asleep twenty minutes later and slept fitfully for the next four hours. When she woke up, they were somewhere over the Atlantic Ocean, and bored, she pulled out the October issue of the UK's *Business Matters* magazine in the seat pocket in front of her. Madeline flipped through the magazine but stopped at the half-page photo of a woman with black hair streaked with gray, one of London's top five female executives. However, Madeline's eyes focused on the Rolex on the woman's left wrist. She looked closely at the watch; it looked like a GMT Master II solid gold Rolex with a graduated bezel. Madeline would love a watch like that for her estate jewelry collection, but that would never happen. A watch like that would be far too expensive. She read the photo caption, "Hannah Davis, Director General of MI5, says her timepiece is a man's watch, 'But it was my father's, so it is precious to me.'"

No doubt it was precious to her, thought Madeline; the gold Rolex was probably worth at least $50,000. She studied Hannah's photo and then set the magazine back in the seat pocket. If she wanted to get her hands on a watch like that for her collection, she'd need an act of God or something.

Madeline nodded off and was able to get another hour of sleep before the plane began its descent.

* * *

London

After Madeline's plane landed, she grabbed her carry-on and groggily made her way to the baggage claim and then with her luggage, she went through the customs line. She walked out of the airport and grabbed one of the glossy black cabs idling out front, and headed off to Heatherwood Hospital.

As the cab drove through the outskirts of London, she just stared out the window, willing it to go faster.

* * *

Ascot, UK

Madeline's cab finally pulled up in front of the Heatherwood Hospital, a somber, three-story building, and she hurried up the steps to the main reception desk with her luggage. The receptionist directed her down a long, quiet corridor to the ICU.

A minute later, Madeline was buzzed into a long room with two rows of patients in narrow hospital beds, hooked up to blinking, humming monitors. It was easy for Madeline to spot Shay at the end of the ICU; her long dark hair was tangled and spread out on a white pillow, an IV in her left arm. Shay's eyes were rimmed in black and blue, and dark bruises ran along her cheekbones and down her neck. A long dark-blue bruise also ran down her left forearm.

As Madeline walked to her bed Shay slowly woke up. Her eyes were a dull, flat brown, the bruises on her cheeks in stark contrast against her pale skin. She tried to smile, "I think somebody told me you were coming today. I'm…glad you are here," she said in a monotone, and winced as she sat up.

Madeline gingerly took her hand. "How do you feel?"

"I feel terrible, and I ache all over and I have a headache too. Other than that, I am apparently all right." Shay looked around the ICU. "There's a lot of beeping sounds in here, constant…beeping. It's noisy here, in a quiet sort of way."

"I'd hug you, but I don't want to hurt you," said Madeline.

"I need a hug," said Shay, so Madeline bent down and hugged Shay carefully.

"I will stay here in the UK," said Madeline, "until you're well enough to leave, which should be soon," and she kissed her sister on the forehead. "Once you are released, I'll take you back to Boston with me for a week or so, just to make sure you're all right."

Madeline pulled a chair closer to the bed and sat down.

"Chip came to see me," said Shay. "He was here for about twenty minutes." She paused, "I don't know, it could have been only five minutes. He told me not to worry about the photo shoot and that it had been postponed. I think I don't remember." Another long pause, and she continued, her voice still flat, "Chip said you would be staying in my suite at the club?"

"Yes," said Madeline, "he was sweet as well as kind, and incredibly gracious. He is also very worried about you. So am I. A doctor here called me at home in the middle of the night last night and told me what had happened, and I flew out as soon as I could get a flight. How awful for you, and I..."

"The doctor wants to run more tests," said Shay. "Sometimes I have double vision too, but the doctor said that would go away. I remember throwing up a lot in the ambulance, which was horrible and was...well, incredibly tacky. Painful too," then she said, "I forgot what I was going to say, I think I was about to say something, but it's gone now."

Shay's eyes closed, and for a moment, Madeline thought Shay had fallen asleep.

"It was all so sudden," said Shay abruptly, and her eyes flashed open, "and very loud, and then I woke up in an ambulance. I don't remember how I got here, in this bed. A policeman asked me a lot of questions, and he told me that Kathleen had died in the accident," and Shay turned her face toward the wall.

Madeline said, "Kathleen was the woman driving the car?"

Shay nodded and turned back toward Madeline. "Is that true, that Kathleen is dead? Is that true?" she asked, tears welling in her eyes.

"Yes, unfortunately, yes, it's true. Kathleen died in the accident. I am so sorry."

Shay wiped away her tears with the back of her right hand, "I told the officer I barely knew her. When I got in her car, Kathleen said she had some totally fascinating information for me, but that's all I remember. Oh, wait, we were going to go to a quiet place in Sunningdale to have dinner and talk about it."

"Talk? Talk about what?"

"She didn't say," said Shay, "or if she did...I don't remember," and her eyes closed again. Shay tried to sit up, but after a couple of seconds, she slumped back down in the bed,

Madeline took Shay's hand again, "I am so sorry for all that has happened. I know it's a big shock and terribly sad. I am glad though that you are alright. What do you mean Kathleen had interesting information? About what?"

"Kathleen?" Shay paused, concentrating, and then she said, "I met her at the library yesterday. The sun was still shining, I think. I told her I was looking for background information on the jewelry theft...from that woman...the Duchess of Windsor. She told me to come back at 6:00 because she said she had something she wanted to show me. I went back at 6:00, and I got in Kathleen's car, and we left." Shay was quiet and then abruptly said, "I just remembered ...when she got in, she handed me a big bag of papers, full of papers. Copies of...something, and she said it was for me."

"Did you see the person who was driving the tow truck?"

"No, I didn't. I started going through the papers that Kathleen gave me, so I didn't see anything until we were hit.

"Well, it is all so tragic," said Madeline. "I am so very sorry. Can I get you anything, like a glass of water or something?"

"No. I can't have anything to drink, or eat, or I'll just throw up again." She nodded to the IV in her left arm, "That's why I'm hooked up to that. The needle hurts when I move my hand."

Madeline bent down and kissed Shay's right hand.

* * *

A minute later, Shay fell asleep. A doctor in blue scrubs walked in the door and introduced himself as Dr. Gene Marley, an older man with a deep voice and kind eyes.

"I was told you had arrived," he said. "Mrs. Wolf is my patient, and you must be her sister, Madeline."

"Yes."

"Your sister sustained a concussion, and she is very bruised. The MRI I had run this morning did show some swelling of the brain, so I will want her to stay in the ICU for observation at least until tomorrow morning. If she is doing well, she can be moved to a regular room. It doesn't seem that she lost consciousness after the accident, which is good news. I'm sure you noticed that your sister is listless, which is common after any brain injury."

"Yes, I noticed that. How serious is her concussion? What about permanent effects?"

"Every concussion is different, and it's too soon to know. Your sister was also severely bruised on her chest, but no ribs were broken. Her injuries are consistent with a T-bone car accident."

Madeline arched her eyebrows, "What is that?"

"That's when the front of one vehicle strikes the side of another, forming the shape of a 'T' at the point of impact."

The doctor's phone buzzed, and he turned away to answer it. He listened for a minute, said "Fine" into the phone, and turned to Madeline. "I have to go. As I said, barring any sudden change, she'll be moved into a private room tomorrow. She does have severe nausea and can't keep anything down, not even water, so she's getting an anti-nausea drug, Ondansetron, through an IV, and she needs to stay on it until the nausea is under control. I can promise you we are doing everything we can for her. I'll talk to you again tomorrow, but she is fine for now. All her vital signs are good," and with a nod, the doctor hurried out of the ICU.

* * *

Ten minutes later, a nurse came up to Shay's hospital bed and said to Madeline,

"We do have limited visitor time in our ICU, only thirty minutes, so I hope you understand that you will have to leave shortly. Also, a policeman wants to speak with Mrs. Wolfe, but her doctor said no, that she needs to sleep. However, I told the officer you were here, and he would like to talk to you, and he's waiting just outside. I hope that was alright."

"Yes of course," said Madeline, and she stepped into the hallway, and an older, good-looking, balding policeman walked up to her.

"I am Detective David Buckingham of the Sunningdale police, and I understand you are Mrs. Wolf's sister. I am investigating the automobile accident, and I have a couple of questions for you. Perhaps we can talk for a few minutes?"

Madeline nodded as he pulled out a folder under his arm and led her to a small alcove off the nurses' station.

"I will do anything to help, but I just flew in from Boston, and I came straight here."

"Did you know Kathleen, the woman who was killed?"

"No, I didn't. Shay told me they had just met at the library and that they were on their way somewhere to have dinner and talk."

"What were they meeting to talk about?"

"Shay said they were going to talk about the Duchess of Windsor's stolen jewelry," and Madeline smiled. "My sister happens to be obsessed with her collection."

Detective Buckingham raised his eyebrows and jotted down a comment in his folder. "The tow truck that struck Mrs. Large's car had been stolen and then abandoned after the accident," he said. "Our forensics team is still checking for fingerprints," he said, "but I am not hopeful. I have several eyewitnesses, not to the accident itself, but just right before. According to them, the tow truck was traveling at a high rate of speed. Do you have any reason to believe anyone would wish to harm your sister, or Mrs. Large?"

"I don't know anything about the librarian, and of course, my sister had only been in Sunningdale for a couple of days, so I can't think of anyone who would wish to harm her. Are you saying this was not an accident?"

"No, not at all," and he shook his head, "we just have to consider all possibilities."

He handed her several photos from his folder, "Ascot's closed-circuit video camera has a couple of surveillance photos of the person breaking into the tow truck when it was parked on a side street. You probably won't recognize him, or her since there are no clear pictures of the face, but I want you to look at it anyway."

Madeline flipped through several photos of a shadowy figure, a soccer cap pulled low over the face, dressed in blue jeans and a t-shirt. A crowbar was in the figure's right hand.

She glanced up at the detective, "A crowbar was used to break in?"

"Yes, not very sophisticated; it's very low-tech, but it is fast and effective," said the detective. "Whoever it was must have been a professional because he or she hot-wired the truck in about a minute. These days, ignition immobilizers make hot wiring difficult, but it's not impossible. Anyway, this thief was good. I have no idea why they would be interested in a tow truck. Maybe because it was a very heavy truck, or maybe because it was just handy? I am canvassing the neighbors to see if there are any additional witnesses. Do call me though if you think of anything that might be helpful, or if your sister remembers any more details about the accident. How is she?"

"The doctor says recovery is a slow process," said Madeline. "I am just glad she is alive."

The detective thanked her and handed Madeline his business card, and after he took down her cellphone number, he left.

Madeline called the Sunningdale Golf Club for a car to pick her up, and while she waited, she sat beside Shay's hospital bed, holding her hand as she slept. Madeline stared at the bruises around Shay's eyes and two dark blue bruises that ran down her cheekbones. Could someone have done this to her sister on purpose? A shiver of fear ran up her neck, but Madeline shook it off, and she kissed Shay's hand goodbye when the car arrived.

* * *

Sunningdale

Twenty minutes later, the club's car took a right at an elegant olive-green sign, *The Sunningdale Golf Club*, and they drove along a narrow, paved road. Madeline stared out the window at elegant brown and white buildings flanked by huge magnolia trees set on immaculate grounds.

The car stopped in front of a rambling three-story building, a small, discreet sign in front that read *The Clubhouse*.

The driver carried Madeline's suitcase up the front steps and into a hushed reception area with a gleaming cherry desk and several matching chairs. She walked across a thick, gray Persian rug up to the desk. She handed the driver a five pound note, but he shook his head and left.

Madeline gave her name to the man at the reception desk, and a tall man in olive-green livery took her carry-on and led her down a hallway of guest suites. Shay's room was the third door down, and after the man unlocked the door, Madeline walked in.

On a black wicker table in the entryway a huge bouquet of yellow tulips stood on a black wicker stand, with a note from Chip. 'Madeline, Welcome to the other side of the pond! How is Shay? Are you available for dinner here tomorrow night at 7:00? Ping me either way.'

She walked into a large living room with huge windows overlooking the eighteenth hole. A gray leather sofa and three chairs, plus two black lacquer side tables, stood in front of the five-foot wide gas fireplace. She turned and saw stainless steel Bosch appliances gleaming in a small kitchen nook, with several chairs clustered around a small ebony table.

In the bedroom, Chinoiserie dressers flanked two queen beds with pale blue silk duvets. From the arched windows in the bedroom, she saw several horses grazing in a small paddock. She walked into a gray marble bathroom. Shay's make-up bag sat on a marble counter with double sinks.

Madeline sat on the bed and sent texts to Abby and Felix that she had seen Shay, who was doing 'as well as could be expected,' and she left a voice mail for Chip, "Thanks for the tulips and the breathtaking suite! I saw Shay ten minutes ago and she was dazed but somewhat coherent. Dinner tomorrow night sounds great. I look forward to meeting you!'

She set her cellphone alarm for 7:00 am UK time. Madeline ordered a green pepper and onion pizza from the club's kitchen, and just as she finished her third piece, there was a knock on her door. She opened it, and a handsome, slender man with dark green eyes walked in. He wore blue jeans, a black turtleneck, and a gold vest.

"I'm Chip," he said with a slow smile that was either seductive or downright thoughtful, depending on the eye of the beholder.

They shook hands and then hugged.

"Hey Madeline, it's good to meet you, I am so sorry that Shay was in such an awful accident. I did take a break and went to see her in the hospital a couple of hours ago. She's a bit banged up, and her speech is slow, and she's groggy, but sort of alright," said Chip.

"She must have been glad to see you," said Madeline. "I went straight from the airport to see her, and then I came here. Yes, she is very bruised, and slow, but she seems to be in good hands at Heatherwood and...

"Unfortunately, Madeline, I need to leave in a minute. I just got word that I have an emergency creative meeting in Paris early tomorrow morning, and I'm flying out tonight, so we can't meet tomorrow night for dinner. The good news is that if Shay has recovered in a couple of weeks and has availability, we will bring her back to the UK as soon as we have a new photoshoot date. I told her about the delay, but I'm not sure if she absorbed it, so you might want to mention it to her again. Sorry, but I must run," and he kissed her goodbye on the cheek and backed out the door, "I'll be in touch."

"Thanks," said Madeline. "And thank you again for the wonderful suite and everything."

Chip nodded and left.

Madeline unpacked her suitcase, changed into a black T-shirt, and fell into bed. Within thirty seconds, she was fast asleep.

Chapter Six

London

L uella sat at her desk at *The Times* in London, staring at her computer screen, running her fingers through her spiky dark hair, her dark brown eyes tight with worry as she worked on the last-minute assignment from her editor. He wanted an article on the Duchess of Windsor's old jewelry theft to run in the newspaper before the anniversary of the damn burglary, including any available update, and Luella was getting nowhere fast. There was some background information available on the Internet, but it was just general information she already knew, and she wasn't about to recycle that for her article. She needed something compelling; she needed a new twist. Something intriguing would work, because she needed to keep her boss, Christopher, a new Features Editor at *The Times*, happy.

The problem was that Christopher was a jackass, an over-educated millennial who was in a rush to be famous before he was thirty. He had complained several times about her writing, which was ridiculous because she was one of the best, if not *the* best, features writer at the newspaper. Christopher had told her that her stories needed more 'flair.' What he really meant was her focus should be on the 'sensational,' as if *The Times* was just another tabloid newspaper but with better sentence structure.

Luella had already read anything recent she could find on the 1946 burglary, which wasn't much; all she learned was that after all these years the police still had zero suspects as well as zero evidence. She took out her cell phone, hit GPS, and tapped in Sunningdale. She'd never been to the town before and after she read about it, the place seemed like every other boring town in the UK that depended on tourism, except that golf tourists tended to have more money. Luella drove home, packed a suitcase, booked a room at the Royal Berkshire Hotel outside of Sunningdale, and was driving down A4 two hours later.

Luella figured she'd start with the local Sunningdale police, which would probably be a waste, but she knew she should start there. Police tend to be suspicious of out-of-town reporters, especially from *The Times*, so as a courtesy it would be good to let them know she was in town. Who knew, they might even have new information on the old theft, one they had never been able to solve, but it would be unwise of her to point that out.

* * *

Sunningdale

Once in Sunningdale, Luella drove straight to the police station. She asked for the chief constable and ten minutes later a gray-haired, heavy-set woman in a gray uniform that was a bit too tight strode out. "How can I help you?" she asked.

The chief constable didn't look helpful; she looked disgruntled, the kind of employee that in the U.S. walks into their place of employment and guns down co-workers. Luella decided her analogy wasn't exactly right; cops didn't shoot other cops, not even in the U.S.

Luella knew the deadline from her boss was ridiculous, and she tamped down a feeling of desperation. She'd already spoken to seven reporters at *The Times*. As far as anyone knew, there had been literally nothing new about the old crime for over eighty years.

"I am a reporter with *The Times*," Luella began. "My name is Luella Kloberdanz, and

I'm writing an update on the Duchess of Windsor jewelry theft in the

1940s because the anniversary is coming up on October 16th. I am hoping you might have some new information on the crime, or perhaps recent background material? Or even better, any new theories about the crime?"

"Oh, that ridiculous burglary. Why does anyone still care about that?" asked the Constable. "The case has been officially closed since 1961, and I have absolutely nothing for you. You are wasting your time, as well as mine. I have more important things to do than talk to a reporter about an old burglary, when the whole world is falling apart, more or less," the officer snapped, and the woman turned and strode back to her office.

Luella wanted to shoot her.

* * *

After Luella left the police station, she went directly to the Sunningdale Golf Club. Inside, the entrance hall had thick, gray Persian run and framed photos of what she assumed were golf celebrities. She walked past a wall of paintings and up to the man standing behind a cherry desk and introduced herself as a *Times* reporter.

"Would it be possible," she asked, "to speak to someone in the housekeeping department who might have heard something about that old jewelry theft in the 1940s, the one that happened next door at the Earl of Dudley's place? I'm writing an article about the old Windsor theft."

"The owner, Jonah Musgrave," said the man at reception, "might have some information for you, but he's away, and I don't know when he will be back, and no, I don't have his number. He can be difficult to get in touch with." The man wrote a name and a phone number on a piece of paper. "Jeff Shovein, who works here, might be able to help you. He may have heard something about that burglary from his father, who was the general manager here in the 1950s and 1960s. Anybody else I can think of for you to talk to is dead, or close to it."

"Thanks," said Luella, glancing at the man's scrawled writing and looking up, "I am also hoping to talk to a maid or a waitress who might have heard something about it over the years. I'm looking for gossip, really. What about your groundskeepers?"

It had been Luella's experience that the staff in upscale hotels and resorts liked to gossip, even if it was very old gossip, which was a lucky thing for reporters all over the world. Since a first-hand source was out of the question, she needed at least a couple of good second- or third-hand sources for her story.

"I can ask around for you, but I doubt any groundskeepers could help you, since they are mostly seasonal. You can ask Jeff about the maids."

Luella stepped outside and called the number.

A man with a low voice answered, "This is Jeff," and she introduced herself as a features writer with *The Times*, explaining she was looking for any new background information on the old Duchess of Windsor theft.

"I'm a three-minute walk away," he laughed. "I'll stop by in a minute."

A not-tall man with merry, brown eyes and a limp walked in shortly after and shook Luella's hand.

"I'm Jeff," he said. "You should really speak to Jonah, the owner. Jonah might be able to tell you something about burglary," said Jeff, quickly adding, "even though the theft happened years before he was born. I say 'might' because he doesn't like to talk about the burglary or talk about anything for that matter. Jonah is a straight arrow, but he doesn't talk much, and he prefers to say as little as possible in any conversation," he glanced at Luella and winked, "Don't tell him I said that. Give me your number, and I'll let him know you would like to speak with him."

"That would be great, thanks," said Luella. "I'm having difficulty finding anyone to talk to. Is there anything surprising that you might have heard about the burglary over the years?" she asked. "I'm just looking for any new and interesting background for my article."

"No, not really," began Jeff. "I do know Jonah used to say his father was consumed by it, as in 'lock, stock and barrel' consumed. I know that years ago his father was convinced the stolen jewelry had been buried somewhere on the grounds here, and he dug up two fairways for God's sake, which must have cost him a bloody fortune," Jeffrey was a man who clearly liked to talk, and he added with another short laugh, "I do remember that Jonah told me once his father said the investigation into the old burglary had been 'compromised by a powerful institution.' Those are his words, not mine."

"That's very interesting, what did you suppose Jonah meant?" said Luella as she scribbled the comment in her notebook.

"I have no idea, and I certainly didn't ask him. Like I said, Jonah says as little as possible in any conversation."

Luella smiled, "I see. I really would love to know more, so it would be great if I could talk to Jonah or his father, just for a minute or two, so please get in touch with them as soon as you can? I am on a tight deadline and would appreciate any help."

"I'm talking to Jonah at 2:00, and I'll let him know, but I can't promise when he'll call back. It might be a while, if ever. You can't talk to his father though, because he died a couple of years ago, God rest his soul."

"Oh, that's too bad, I would have liked to speak with him," said Luella, and realized that sounded heartless. "I didn't mean that the way it sounded. I meant to say I'm just sorry he died."

"We all were. His father loved to fish, and he drowned in a sudden squall on the Bull River. I don't think Jonah ever got over it, if you want my opinion."

Luella smiled sympathetically. "What is he like?" she asked. She could tell that unlike his boss, Jonah, Jeff was a man who liked to talk.

Jeff said, "Jonah? He is a very rich man and a very busy one, too, but he's a good guy and easy to work for. He owns five other golf clubs in the UK and a couple of big hotel chains in France. He's also very wrapped up with his charities, so he's away a lot. That's why he's so hard to get ahold of."

Luella thanked Jeff and headed back to her car. She knew digging up new information wouldn't be easy, but it was now looking to be impossible. Although, what did she expect to find, following up on a decades-old crime? She was afraid she wouldn't hear back from Jonah before her deadline, given the 'prefers to say as little as possible' part. She was worried; she had no idea where to even start with her article.

As Luella drove back to her hotel, she thought about her options. People in the UK like to read stories about the lifestyles of the royals, and if something criminal is involved, the interest level is off the charts. What should her angle be? Perhaps she should concentrate on the duke and duchess's Scotland Yard bodyguards while they were in Sunningdale? The bodyguards would both be dead by now, of course, but maybe she could write a human-interest profile on each of them, reporting on what they did before the theft, and then give a bit of news about their lives after their brief brush with royalty. Luella knew how to write a compelling story; after all, she had managed to make Brexit sound interesting and almost sexy for three years.

First, though, she should find out their names and where they stayed when they were off duty in Sunningdale. Maybe Basil could help her with that? It should be easy for him to find out since MI5 and Scotland Yard both reported to the Home Secretary.

She texted Basil, "Sorry for the bother, but I am trying to get the names of the Scotland Yard bodyguards for the Windsor's and where they stayed when they were in Sunningdale. It would be very helpful if I could get that information. Could you please check to see if you can find that information for me? It would be great if you could find it, or if you don't have it, could you possibly let me know where I might look?"

She went back to her computer and scrolled through the endless articles written right after the theft. The eleventh article was a five-page account of the theft, with the last page devoted to rumors about the burglary, which was great. Her boss, Christopher, loved rumors. The most interesting rumor she had just read would create a sensation, even today, which Christopher would love. The story was that before the Abdication, when the Duke of Windsor had been King Edward VIII, he had given Mrs. Simpson about twenty pieces of jewelry that didn't belong to him personally but instead belonged to the Crown; jewelry that should have stayed in the UK with the new king and his wife, the new queen. Instead, the rumor was that the jewelry was taken out of the country by the now ex-king, and he gave them to his infamous wife, the Duchess of Windsor.

Then, ten years later, according to the old article, the duke and duchess returned to the UK in 1946 for the first time since the Abdication. Unfortunately, the duchess brought those pieces of jewelry that belonged to the Crown with her for their short visit to Sunningdale, a visit where that jewelry was suddenly and mysteriously stolen.

Included in the article was information on Scotland Yard's investigation, headed by no less than the Assistant Commissioner of Scotland Yard, R.M. Howe. Luella found it surprising that such a high-ranking official ran an investigation of what was basically just a burglary, plus one that was never solved.

The article ended by speculating that Scotland Yard itself, under the supervision of MI5, had carried out the theft in Sunningdale on behalf of Buckingham Palace to get the Crown Jewels back from 'that woman', the Duchess of Windsor.

Seriously interesting, thought Luella, but it was just old speculation, nothing but a rumor, and she couldn't use it in her article.

Then she thought about it; maybe, just maybe, she could use it. Yes, she could make it work. She could mention it as an 'old theory' that had been raised right after the theft, and then she could list the reasons why it was still a credible solution to the old crime. Yes, now that she thought about it, she could work with that.

Luella knew she would have to go with it, because her deadline was coming up and she had nothing else, absolutely nothing.

* * *

Ascot

Late that afternoon, after a twelve-hour sleep in the club's luxurious suite in Sunningdale, Madeline went to the hospital in Ascot and stopped at the nurses' station. A nurse told her that Shay had been moved out of the ICU to a private room, #511, on the fifth floor.

On the drive to the hospital, Madeline worked out her daily routine in the UK; in the mornings, she would visit Shay at the hospital, and the rest of the day, Madeline would be in her room at the clubhouse, talking with Abby about Coda Gems' daily sales, as well contacting gem dealers for her estate jewelry collection. So far, she had locked in only three more pieces of jewelry. She wondered if she was wasting her time, then dismissed the thought. Her luck would be sure to change.

The elevator door opened, and she sighed. Her days would be full.

"You're still here in the UK?" Shay asked slowly when Madeline walked into her hospital room.

"Where else would I be?" said Madeline, pulling up a chair. "You're my sister; somebody has to look after you, and that somebody is me."

Shay stared at her, then finally said, "There is nothing to do here but sleep."

"Sleep will help you recover," said Madeline.

Shay closed her eyes and turned toward the wall, but Madeline couldn't tell if she was sleeping or not. After half an hour, she decided Shay was sleeping, so Madeline wrote her a note and left.

* * *

The next day, when Madeline arrived at the hospital, a nurse showed her the front page of a small, local paper, the *Ascot & Eaton Express,* with an article about Kathleen's death on the front page. The reporter had obviously spoken with someone from Kathleen's family, and Shay's name was even mentioned in a brief, gossipy sidebar to the article.

The sidebar read:

> *In the car with Kathleen was Mrs. Shay Wolf, her good friend visiting from the U.S. This reporter was told by the family that Kathleen was happy that day because she had just discovered information about an old royal honor surprisingly awarded years ago to a law enforcement officer, and the two women were on their way to dinner to talk about it when Kathleen's car was hit by the tow truck. Mrs. Wolf, who was injured in the accident, is recovering at Heathwood Hospital and is expected to fly back to the U.S. in four or five days.*

"I'll tell Shay she made the local news," Madeline to the nurse, "although I would hardly call her and Kathleen 'good friends' since they just met. It sounds like someone spoke to the family."

The nurse laughed and said, "You know how reporters are," and Madeline took the elevator up to Shay's room. She knew exactly how reporters were. Felix was always tracking down sources for his stories, and he didn't care who they were or who they were related to.

Madeline knocked and went in Shay's room. She was sitting up in bed staring out the window through half-shut, swollen eyes, her IV pole, as usual, next to her bed.

"I hope you like your room?" asked Madeline. "It's very nice."

Shay ignored her.

"How are you feeling?" she asked, but Shay did not respond. "I asked, how are you feeling?" repeated Madeline.

"I am not sure, alright, I guess," sighed Shay. "Maybe just sort of alright. Or maybe I feel just fine. I can't tell the difference. Is it morning?"

"Yes, it's 9:00 am."

"I am tired," said Shay, stretched out in the bed and closed her eyes, "I don't feel like talking."

"I thought you'd like to know I read an article today about the accident and Kathleen."

Shay's eyes opened wide, and she sat up in bed, "I liked Kathleen. She was very smart and quick, you know? She was one of the smartest women I've ever met."

"Your name was in the newspaper, too," said Madeline.

"That's nice," she said, and went back to staring vacantly out the window, and showed no interest in reading the article.

"Do you want to watch TV?" asked Madeline.

Shay didn't respond, just continued staring out the window.

A doctor stopped in to see Shay five minutes later, but by then, she was asleep.

Madeline followed him out the doorway and down the hallway, "I'm worried about Shay. She is so withdrawn and is just not herself."

"Each concussion is different," the doctor said to Madeline, "but it is not unusual for patients to be very passive and listless after a concussion. Her brain needs time to recover from the trauma."

Madeline wanted to ask, "But what if that doesn't happen?" but she didn't.

The doctor reassured Madeline, "The good news is that the last MRI of your sister's brain did show improvement."

Madeline thanked him, turned around and went back down the corridor to Shay's room. Chip stopped by to visit Shay and stayed for twenty minutes. Shay didn't say much and didn't seem to be following Madeline and Chip's conversation, but at least she stayed awake while Chip was there.

* * *

The Patron assumed the immediate threat of the librarian's unfortunate discovery of a clue to 1947 royal award for personal service had disappeared with her death in the tow truck crash. However, once the Patron read the sidebar article in the *Ascot & Eaton Express* there was an initial sense of panic that was tamped down by caution. It would probably turn out to be nothing, but at the very least it was concerning.

The Patron looked down at the name again in the newspaper, a Mrs. Shay Wolf. The woman might or might not become a threat, since it was impossible to know precisely what she had learned from the librarian. However, it was better to wait until this Shay Wolf woman was released from the hospital and monitor her activities.

* * *

Madeline walked into Shay's hospital room that afternoon. Shay sat up, gingerly rubbing the sleep from her eyes. "There's always people dashing about here," she said, "like there's a fire or something."

"It's a hospital; that's what people do. How are you?" asked Madeline.

Shay stared out her window at a rushing river below. Her bruises had faded but were still noticeable.

"I'm glad you are here," said Shay. "I want to leave today."

"Soon, you can leave soon, just not today."

Shay sighed, "When can I leave? My ribs are killing me, and I want to leave. It's very boring here." She turned her head to the wall and was asleep within five minutes.

An hour later Madeline whispered, "I have to go now," to the still sleeping Shay. "I'll see you tomorrow," and she kissed Shay on the cheek, avoiding the bruises, and went down the hall to the elevator.

Chapter Seven

London

B asil was at his desk, getting ready to go home, when his phone rang. He didn't recognize the phone number, but since Hannah used constantly changing burner phones, he answered every call from an unknown number.

He answered immediately, "This is Basil,"

"Why is the press snooping around Sunningdale asking questions about the Duchess of Windsor burglary?" Hannah demanded.

"They are?"

"You should already know that, since I told you to be on the alert," said Hannah. "A reporter from *The Times*, Luella Kloberdanz, has been asking the staff at the Sunningdale Golf Club, which, as you may recall, is next door to the scene of the crime, about any recent rumors they may have heard about that Duchess of Windsor theft. Which is exactly what I don't want to happen. I have someone pulling a dossier together on this reporter now."

Basil almost asked Hannah how she was able to have a dossier pulled on anyone since she was officially retired from MI5, but he didn't. Instead, he said to her, "Luella sent me a text a couple of days ago."

"You know this reporter? You know her?" said Hannah, her voice now cold.

"Yes, but not well. I met her at a couple of the Brexit press conferences when they were at #10 Downing Street, and we talked a fair amount. She called me the other day looking for background information about the Windsor theft. It turns out she was assigned to write a story about it since the anniversary is coming up, and because I'm with MI5, she thought I might know someone at Scotland Yard who was at least officially in charge of the investigation. I was polite, of course, when I told her I couldn't help her. Don't worry though; she is harmless."

"Don't be dense Basil, reporters are never harmless. Why was this woman in touch with you in the first place?"

"I don't know, maybe because I'm the only person she knows that is connected to Scotland Yard? Her editor told her to write an article about the 1946 theft, which will likely be some sort of puff piece. She has no experience in crime reporting, so I didn't think it merited any...."

"Dammit, Basil, you should have told me the moment you heard from her! I told you to be on the alert. I can't believe you didn't think to let me know...anyway, call her back immediately and find out what she's up to and let me know. I want you to get friendly with her, stay close while she's 'doing research' in Sunningdale, and keep me posted. Please.

"I just want this case to be permanently closed; for my father's sake, God rest his soul." Hannah then added, as an afterthought, "While you're chatting, ask her if she thinks the jewelry is still in the UK."

Hannah hung up with no goodbye, just a click, and she was gone.

When he and Hannah had lunch at the Blue Cardinal, she had sounded certain the jewels had been taken out of the country. Now, it seemed that Hannah thought they were still in the UK. Why was she being cagey? He left for a long lunch with an Oxford classmate, tired of wondering about the old theft. Who cared after all these years?

* * *

After lunch, Basil sat at his desk thinking. Hannah expected him to get back to Luella, so he needed to call her. Since she had asked him for information on the bodyguards, he thought he had read something about where they had stayed in Sunningdale, so he went through the thick file and found it ten minutes later. The bodyguards' names were in the file as well, but for security reasons, he knew he couldn't give that information to Luella. The names of bodyguards are considered strictly confidential by the UK's intelligence agencies, and their names are never publicly released. With any luck, he thought Luella would be happy just to know where they stayed. Besides, thought Basil, why did she need their names anyway?

He sent her a text, "Hi Luella, my apologies, but I've been out of town, and I just now saw your message. I do have a couple of old files on the burglary, and I was able to dig up where the bodyguards stayed. Call me, and let's get together and talk."

The timing was perfect because Hannah had told him to get close to Luella. More to the point, he wanted to talk to Luella and find out if she believed the Duchess' jewelry was still in the UK. Hannah would be pleased with any information he could give her.

Luella called him back five minutes later.

"Thanks for getting back to me," she began.

"No problem. I thought it would be best if we met. How does your schedule for this week look?"

"It's a little crazy," said Luella. "I'm in Sunningdale now, and I've been talking to people, or rather trying to talk to people. Can you just give me your bodyguard information over the phone?"

"I'd rather talk to you in person," said Basil. "If you fill me in on what you're finding, and any thoughts you have on the theft, that would be helpful for my file. Do you think her jewelry is still in the UK? That would be good for me to know. We really should talk because I also think I may be able to connect any dots for you in your article."

A pause, and Luella said, "Well, I would like your opinion on several statements in my article, so send me a couple of times that you're available over the next day or so. I will be in London tomorrow night," she said, "but I will…"

"Then let's meet and…"

"Sorry, but I'm coming in just for a very late dinner with a friend at the *Telegraph*, and after that I need to take the 11:00 train back to Sunningdale.

Let's talk tomorrow around 9:00? I'll have to move a couple of things on my calendar to meet, but I'll be happy to do that…" and then she added, "I'm curious, have you been in touch with Jonah Musgrave? He's a mysterious guy, not very easy to reach."

"No, Jonah hasn't returned my calls."

"Mine neither," said Luella, and they both laughed and then Luella had to take another call.

* * *

Sunningdale

Shortly after, Luella's cellphone on the desk of her hotel room buzzed with the arrival of a text. She glanced at her phone; it was from Christopher, her editor.

"I need a three or four-sentence teaser for your burglary anniversary article ASAP please, and I need to have it in the next hour. I need to include it in my new 'Upcoming Feature's Alert' to promote your Windsor burglary article. The teaser will run tomorrow."

She picked up her phone and called him, "Thanks Christopher, a teaser is a wonderful idea, but I'm still working on the story, still firming things up. I can send something to you in a day or two. My article is about a theory, based on an old rumor at the time, but no proof, it's just an old rumor."

"Two days won't work, I'm sorry, I need a teaser from you today," he said. "Could you send me a couple of sentences shortly, as in the next fifteen minutes? As for the article itself, a theory will be fine so long as you couch it as your 'thoughtful questions' about the theft. I need something dramatic, make it as dramatic as possible, and as soon as possible."

"You mean you want something 'sensational?'" she said.

"You know what I mean."

"And the teaser runs tomorrow?"

"Yes, tomorrow."

"Can't you hold off for…"

"No, I can't, I don't have a choice. A teaser for your story has to run in tomorrow's paper because the managing editor is ready to fill the space he's holding for your article if it doesn't. Sorry for the pressure, but it can't be helped."

Luella emailed three sentences off to Christopher ten minutes later, "Watch for Luella Kloberdanz's article next Thursday, with thoughtful questions on the still unsolved Duchess of Windsor's jewelry theft in Sunningdale years ago. Be sure to read her surprising resurrection of an old theory: was the investigation of the famous robbery compromised from the beginning by a powerful institution?"

Christopher called her immediately, "Luella, this is great, just what I'm looking for! Good job, this is terrific, it's terrific! I'm just double checking that you are comfortable if I go with this."

Luella hesitated, and then slowly said "Yes, you can go ahead with it," and Christopher hung up.

Still, Luella was uneasy, was her teaser too bold? She was going out on a limb with it, although her article was basically just gossip which of course she had positioned as 'speculation'. She called Jeff Shovein to see if he had told Jonah she needed to talk to him. After all, Jeff had given her the 'compromised by a powerful institution' quote, from Jonah's father.

"It's Luella from *The Times*," she said when Jeff answered, "You were going to leave Jonah a message to call me, but he never did, and I urgently need to run something past him. Could you give me his number?"

"Unfortunately, I can't give his number out. I did leave him a message to call you."

Luella sighed, "Could you please leave him another one and say it's urgent, very urgent? Tell him need his opinion on my teaser that will run in *The Times* tomorrow about an article I'm writing on the Duchess of Windsor burglary. If he has a comment, of any kind, he needs to call me tonight. I will text you the copy now. It's very short, only three sentences. But Jonah must read it right away tonight, in case I need to make any changes, so it's very important that I speak with him. Can you let me know as soon as you can if you've been able to reach him?"

"Jonah doesn't like to talk about that old burglary," said Jeffrey. "I guess he got tired of it or something. I'm sorry, but I'll do the best I can," and he disconnected.

Chapter Eight

Sunningdale

A bby called Madeline early that afternoon, sounding exhausted and hoarse.

"Madeline, you won't believe it, but I have pneumonia of all things, and I know this is very last minute, but the owner of Neptune Gems, Aaron Heath, just called. He's in New York for Jewelry Week, and he wants to stop in Boston tomorrow on his way back to California and do a walk-through of our store. He is sounding very interested in buying Coda Gems."

"What? You have pneumonia, and this guy Aaron wants to come to the store tomorrow?" said Madeline, surprised, and not happy.

From her hospital bed, Shay looked at Madeline questioningly, so Madeline hit the speakerphone.

"Yes," said Abby, "I have a temperature of 103, a bad cough, and I've been to the doctor, and no, it's not COVID, but I do have pneumonia and the timing couldn't be worse. Aaron and I have been talking about doing a walk-through of Coda Gems in two weeks, but now he and his CFO want to stop in Boston tomorrow. Tomorrow! He did apologize that it's so last minute, but he said it was important."

"He wants to come to Boston," repeated Madeline.

"Madeline," said Abby gently, "I know you don't want to sell Coda, but he is very interested. Aaron just wants to see the store, so I think he should come and have a look. The least we can do is listen to what he has to say."

85

"But I'm still trying to find…" began Madeline.

Abby interrupted, "I know, but we can't pass up this opportunity with Neptune Gems, since who knows what will happen with your estate jewelry idea? I'm sorry, Madeline, but I just don't think it can be pulled together soon enough. That's why we need to be open to what Aaron will have to say. He wants to come tomorrow, and I can't meet him, so would you…could you possibly come back to Boston tomorrow just for the day? Martin will be at the store, of course, tomorrow, but as owners, one of us should be there to meet him, and I just can't. So could you please fly back just for a day?"

Madeline froze. Flying to Boston to meet with a prospective buyer of Coda Gems was the last thing she wanted to do, but she could hardly say no, so she didn't.

"Abby, yes of course I will come back to Boston tomorrow," and she shot a look at Shay, listening intently from her bed. "I'm not in my room at the golf club," said Madeline. "I'm at the hospital with Shay and…."

"Thanks, Madeline," sighed Abby, "I really appreciate your coming back. Hold on, and I'll check on early morning flights for you from London to Boston right now."

Madeline was on hold for ten minutes, and she anxiously doodled on a hospital message pad, not able to believe a prospective buyer wanted to do a walk-through of Coda Gems.

Finally, Abby came back on the line, "Flights to Boston tomorrow morning are all booked, but I just reserved a ticket for you on Delta's last flight out tonight. I know it's extremely short notice, but I'll email you your itinerary as soon as I hang up, including your return flight to London tomorrow night. I am sure that Shay will be in good hands at the hospital."

"I appreciate your setting up my flights. Shay is in a great hospital, so she'll be just fine," and Madeline smiled and looked over at Shay.

"I appreciate your making the trek," said Abby, "and again, big thanks!"

"No problem, we're partners. I'll text you when I land in Boston tonight," said Madeline, "and I'll be at the store tomorrow in plenty of time for the two o'clock meeting. Whatever happens, whatever is the right thing to do, we'll just do it. Don't worry, I will make sure Aaron sees whatever he wants to see, and most importantly, I will make sure he is impressed, because we do have a beautiful store. The two of us created a beautiful store, didn't we?"

"Yes, we did, Madeline. Thank you, I really appreciate this, and...." Abby started coughing, and Madeline waited until she caught her breath.

"Have a good flight. Goodbye," ended Abby and hung up.

Madeline turned to Shay, "I need to leave now and pack, but I'll be gone for just a little over a day. You'll be fine."

Shay's smile was tepid, but she didn't say anything.

Madeline called the club and asked for a car to be sent immediately, and she picked up her bag, "Call me, day or night, if you need anything," she said to Shay.

Madeline kissed the top of Shay's head and hurried out the door. When Madeline turned around at the door to blow a kiss to her, Shay was staring out the window at the hospital's parking lot.

* * *

Flight to Boston

Three hours later, Madeline boarded a Delta flight to Boston, wearing jeans and a University of Iowa sweatshirt. Her carry-on with a change of clothes and as well as her laptop were stowed in the overhead bin. A biography of FDR was in her shoulder bag, but she was too distracted to read. She fell asleep somewhere over the Atlantic Ocean and slept for three hours, and then she was wide awake. She turned on an overhead light and tried to read a magazine but couldn't concentrate. She was restless, wrapped up with sad thoughts of Coda Gems.

Five very long hours later, the plane landed at Logan. Exhausted, Madeline walked into Boston's arrivals' terminal, and thought she heard a familiar voice call her name.

She turned, and Felix walked up to her, saying, "My car is in the lot down the street. I'll drive you home."

"How did you know that I…"

Felix took her carry-on and laptop case out of her hand, "Shay called me and said you were flying out of London this evening on Delta's last flight to Boston. Since I am, after all, an investigative reporter, I figured out which one you'd be on. So here I am, at your service."

Madeline was exhausted and kissed him on the cheek, and they walked out of the terminal. She noticed he picked up her carry-on and pulled it behind him while she carried her laptop bag and purse, just like in the old days.

"Are you hungry?" said Felix as they walked to his car.

"I'm too tired to eat," she said, "I just want to go home."

Ten minutes later, they were in his car driving through the Sumner Tunnel. He turned to her at a stop light, "I am very glad to see you," he said.

"Felix, thank you for doing this. It is very kind of you, very thoughtful, but you didn't need to meet me."

"No worries. I figured this was the only way I would get to see yo, since Shay told me you would be in Boston for less than a day for a big meeting, and God knows, the way things are going, when I would get to see you again. So, of course, I had to come. Shay said there's a guy who is thinking of buying Coda Gems?"

"Yes. If he likes what he sees, he might make us an offer," and Madeline turned her head and stared out the passenger window.

"This must be very hard for you," he said, glancing at her as he cut off a city bus to merge onto I-93.

"Yes, it is. It is very hard."

"You've been very busy with Coda Gems lately. Although Madeline, to be honest, you've always been busy with your store since I've known you. It takes up a lot of your time, most of your time, it seems."

"Life is busy. There is always something that comes up."

"So, now the shoe is on the other foot?" he said, glancing at her out of the corner of his eye.

"What is that supposed to mean?" she said sharply.

Madeline fell asleep as Felix drove through downtown Boston and she didn't wake up until he pulled up in front of her condo building at 25 Channel

Center. He parked in the visitor section and came around to the passenger side, picked up her carry-on again, and they walked inside.

* * *

Boston

In the elevator Madeline hit the button for the 11th floor, and she slid her key in the lock of her door, and Felix followed her inside. She blearily went into the bedroom and sat down on the bed to take off her shoes, leaned back and pulled the covers over her for a moment because she felt chilly, and then she fell asleep.

Madeline woke up from a deep sleep five hours later. The covers pulled up to her chin. Felix lay next to her, wide awake and watching her. She glanced under the covers; she was still in her jeans and a sweatshirt; she really had been exhausted.

Felix smiled, "I meant to just lie beside you for a minute last night before I left, watching you sleep, but I nodded off. I see you still sleep with your mouth open."

Madeline gave him an annoyed look and glanced at her cellphone on the bedside table, and she checked the time. "It's 8:30 am," she said, "I have to take a shower and leave for the store."

Felix kissed her on the cheek, "It was wonderful to spend the night, well, part of the night, with you. What time do you have to be at the store? We can have breakfast at that restaurant, The Contessa, across the street from your store, if you have time."

Felix sat up, yawning. Madeline could see his white shirt on the floor, and she looked under the covers again. He was still in his blue jeans.

Madeline got out of bed, "Well, yes, I suppose I have time for breakfast. I just want to be at the store no later than 10:00. Martin will have already been at the store for more than an hour, so he'll have the jewelry displays all set up, but I'll want to triple-check everything before Neptune arrives at

2:00. I'll take a quick shower now."

"I need to get coffee and make a couple of calls. I'll be back in less than an hour," he said, heading to the door.

"Bring a coffee for me? The usual." Madeline grabbed her make-up and garment bag out of her carry-on and slipped into the bathroom.

Forty-five minutes later, Madeline was ready, her short, curly blonde hair pulled back with black combs and dressed in a cashmere black dress and a pair of low black heels. She felt like she was going to a funeral, which was true in a way, since she was on her way to a meeting that was likely to be the beginning of the end of Coda Gems. She could feel tears gather in the corner of her eyes. She brushed them away when Felix walked in the door and handed her a cup of coffee.

"You never wear a dress," was all he said.

"You're a writer," she said, "you should have just said I look glamorous and left it at that."

"Of course, what was I thinking?" he said, and the two left her condo and parted on the sidewalk for their cars.

* * *

Twenty-five minutes later, they met at the Contessa, the restaurant in the Newbury Hotel. They took a table by a huge window that looked out on Newbury Street, directly across the street from Coda Gems' front door.

"I can't believe Shay called you last night to tell you I was flying into Boston," said Madeline. "She shouldn't have done that."

Felix laughed, "Shay said that's what big sisters do. I was hoping you'd be glad to see me, and I think you were."

Madeline smiled, "It was a surprise, and it was very sweet of you to come to the airport."

"I was happy to see you walk off the plane."

A waiter came up and took their order. Madeline ordered an omelet and Felix ordered his usual, two eggs sunny side up, three links of sausage, and coffee, black of course. The man lived on caffeine, eggs, and sausage.

"How is Shay?" said Felix. "When she called me last night, I asked her how she was doing, and she mumbled something about being tremendously bored. I noticed her speech was a little slow."

Felix's phone rang, and he looked at the caller ID. He abruptly stood up and walked to a window. He spoke animatedly for five minutes while Madeline scrolled through her text messages. When Felix came back to the table, his blue eyes were shadowed.

"Something has come up, and I am so sorry Madeline, but unfortunately, I must leave right away. One of my new sources, a woman who is a security analyst on an LNG tanker out of China, has just been arrested in Everett for a visa violation and is in jail, which is ridiculous, and of course, she is upset. I need to talk to the Everett police and get it straightened out, and I'm not sure how long I'll be. I'll call you later and meet up with you."

Felix kissed Madeline on the cheek, signaled the waiter, and paid the bill. As he was leaving, he turned and waved goodbye to Madeline.

Madeline stared after him, struck by a feeling of deja vu. She should have known something like this would happen. Even so, she never had become used to it.

After she finished her omelet, a text arrived from Felix, "So sorry I had to leave, I hope your meeting goes well. I'll call you."

She dropped her phone back in her pocket. She didn't care if he called, or if he didn't.

* * *

Madeline crossed Newbury Street, crowded with honking cars and jay-walking pedestrians and she walked up to Coda Gems' plate glass front window. She stared at their logo, a dazzling laser-cut ruby bracelet set against a black velvet background. Before they opened the store on Newbury Street, it had taken her and Abby two weeks to decide on an Arial Black font for their elegant logo. Madeline ran her fingers across the lettering, still so beautiful. It would always be beautiful in her mind's eye. She pulled the handle of their heavy glass door and walked in.

Inside, Martin was waiting for her, his dark hair slicked back, but instead of designer jeans and a Versace shirt, today he wore a black suit, a stark-white shirt, and a red bow tie. However, his shoes, as usual, were black patent leather.

"Abby told me you were flying in to meet with the Neptune Gem people today," said Martin, "and I'm glad you are here. I saw her at the store yesterday, before she went to the doctor, and she did not look well at all, so it's good she's recovering at home. You, on the other hand, look lovely, and in a dress no less, but no cowboy boots? I'm surprised."

"And you, my dear Martin," she said, "look like Fred Astaire in "Flying Down to Rio." Martin just stared at her, and she explained, "It's a musical from the 1930s. It was a big hit back then, with lots of dancing, the cheek-to-cheek kind."

Martin grabbed his umbrella from the closet and, laughing, broke into a 'shim sham shimmy' tap dance routine, "Don't be silly, of course, I know the movie," said Martin, "I wore the wrong shoes today though, because tap-dancing doesn't work if you don't have cleats."

Madeline laughed as she applauded, "It was a wonderful routine anyway, my dear Martin. I am glad to see you."

Martin bowed low, "I know this is a big day for you and Abby," he said, "and I hope all goes well with Neptune, but of course, I don't want you to sell the store. To be honest, I hope they hate you, and hate me too, of course, and that they detest the store. Oh, Madeline, I will be so sad to lose this dear place, deeply, sadly, in perpetual perpetuity, and I…"

"I get it Martin, and I feel the same. However, we do need to be enthusiastic today for Abby."

"Of course. Don't worry, I can do 'enthusiastic,' no problem."

Madeline walked around their four glass display cases, and said, "I just had a great idea, let's move all the ruby jewelry to the front glass case, and focus the spotlights on them. I just think it will be better, more striking, don't you agree? Rubies after all are very dramatic."

Martin agreed, and twenty minutes later, the switch had been made. Their ruby rings, bracelets, earrings, and four ruby necklaces glowed under the

LED spotlights.

"That was a good idea," said Martin, "I love it. The rubies look fantastic."

Over the next hour, several customers came into the store to make small purchases, and then Madeline received a text on her cell phone. She said to Martin, "I just got an alert from Aaron at Neptune. Their plane is delayed, and they won't be here until sometime after 3:00."

A few more customers came in over the lunch hour, and one purchased a two-carat diamond ring and another a gold Tiffany bracelet, but after that, the store was quiet, and the time dragged. Madeline and Martin re-arranged the gleaming jewelry in the ruby glass case once again, and Madeline said, "Great, now it's perfect! My sister Shay fell in love with this ring," she said, picking up the Cartier ruby ring and holding it in her hand, "until she saw a photo of a Burmese ruby ring which stole her heart."

"Everyone needs their heart stolen," said Martin, and he pulled out his cell phone. "You know what? Since we have a couple more hours to wait, I think what we need is a little music," he clicked on Spotify, hit a couple more buttons, and the sound of Glen Miller's 1940s swing classic "In the Mood" with its hypnotic riffing filled the store. Martin turned up the volume, took Madeline's hand, his other hand on the small of her back, and the two slid across the floor in a graceful foxtrot, their steps slow-slow, quick-quick, and Madeline laughed out loud.

Martin turned up the volume on Spotify even louder, and for another twenty minutes, the two danced to more Glen Miller, the reason Madeline didn't hear her cellphone chime with a text, and neither she nor Martin heard their front door open. A tall, handsome man in a navy suit abruptly came up behind Martin and tapped him on the shoulder mid-step. Martin looked up, surprised, and after he stepped back, the man took Madeline's hand, his left hand on her back.

"I am Aaron Heath from Neptune, and you must be Madeline. At the last minute, we were able to catch an earlier flight, and we just landed, but obviously, my text didn't get to you. He said laughing, "The timing is perfect, because I never could pass up the chance for a little foxtrot."

For the next five minutes, he gracefully danced Madeline around and then in between Coda Gems' four cases of jewelry in a graceful foxtrot, this time to the sounds of Glen Miller's" 'Tuxedo Junction.'

Only then did she notice an older man in a dark blue suit standing near the door, smiling as he watched Madeline and Aaron glide across the store. Aaron nodded in the man's direction and said to Madeline, "He's with me," and he introduced Neptune Gems' CFO.

When the song ended, Aaron kissed her hand, "Thank you, I haven't danced the foxtrot for at least twenty years."

The men from Neptune stayed at Coda Gems for over two hours that afternoon, examining their inventory in the glass cases and their walk-in safe, and then Madeline took Aaron and his CFO on a tour of their Back Bay neighborhood of upper Newbury Street.

* * *

After the tour, the Neptune team and Madeline walked back into the store, and Aaron checked his watch. "We need to leave now for our flight to Los Angeles. Thank you, Madeline, for your time. You are lovely, your store is lovely, your inventory is excellent, and you answered all my questions. Plus, you are also a terrific dancer. I will be in touch with Abby."

He shook hands with Madeline, then with Martin, and then the two men from Neptune Gems walked out the door.

Madeline and Martin stared at each other, and Martin said, "Now that was a great way to say goodbye to Coda Gems."

Madeline shook her head, "No, it wasn't a goodbye. Let's just call it a 'thank you' to the store. It has been a good and wonderful place for me and Abby, and for you as well."

"Of course," said Martin, "you are right."

She called Abby, but she didn't pick up, so Madeline left a voicemail, "Aaron Heath and his CFO have come and gone. The walk-through went well, and he was very impressed with our store. He said he'd be in touch with you. Feel better!"

Madeline walked up to her hapless sago palm by the window. The sago palm was still alive, and she was glad it seemed to be doing all right without her, well, sort of all right.

* * *

At Logan Airport two hours later as, Madeline waited to board her plane for London Abby still hadn't called, but Felix had.

"I am so sorry I bolted out of the restaurant," he said, "but I was happy I saw you; even though it was short, it was sweet."

"Yes, it was short, "she said. The conversation unpleasantly reminded Madeline of conversations with Felix when they'd been married. She quickly added, "I do appreciate the pickup at the airport and for breakfast. Thank you again."

"I was glad to see you. Let me know when you'll be coming home."

"Yes, of course," she said. "I hope you got your source from the oil tanker in Everett out of jail?"

"Yes, she's out on bail. The charge will probably be dropped in a day or so, which is good news. I was thinking…"

"Sorry, I have to go," said Madeline, "I have a call coming in from Abby. We'll talk soon," she said and disconnected.

Abby wasn't calling, Madeline just wanted to end the conversation with Felix, because it was a familiar one, in a bad way. She just wanted to get back to the UK and see Shay. At least Madeline had a book to read on the plane since sleep was out of the question. She checked her message; there was only one. The dealer who had told her he was willing to consign the beautiful 24kt gold Harry Winston mesh bracelet called to let her know he had just sold it to a buyer in Dubai.

After she listened to the dealer's message three times, she ordered a double shot of gin from an airport bar and drained it in less than a minute. As she stared out the airport window, it started to rain hard, a depressing, unforgiving rain. She boarded the plane, knowing she would get little sleep.

* * *

London

The next morning, Luella's teaser ran on the front page of *The Times* in their "Upcoming Features Alert." As usual, the Patron received a copy of *The Times* delivered before the mass distribution of the paper's print, and the online version was available. The Patron glanced at the gold Rolex on the bedside stand and smiled; the newspaper was on time as usual.

The Patron picked up the newspaper and read Luella's teaser, and the smile disappeared. The Patron made three cell phone calls, each of them short.

* * *

Shortly after 6:00 a.m., Basil's cellphone rang. He was in bed, asleep, but he woke up quickly. It was Hannah, and she was not happy.

"Have you seen *The Times*?" she demanded.

"No, not yet. What's up?"

Hannah read the teaser out loud, "'Watch for Luella Kloberdanz's article next Thursday, with thoughtful questions on the unsolved Duchess of Windsor jewelry theft. Be sure to read it for her surprising resurrection of an old theory: Was the investigation into the famous robbery compromised from the beginning by a powerful institution?'"

"I want to know what this Luella woman means. Basil, this is a disaster This is exactly what I did not want to have happen, and now it has happened."

"I have no idea what she is talking about," said Basil quickly. "I spoke to her yesterday, and she didn't mention anything about a teaser for her article in today's paper. I know she's in London having dinner with friends, and then she's going straight back to Sunningdale tonight on the 11:00 train. The good news is I'll be meeting her tomorrow for lunch at the restaurant Hawksmoor Borough, which is at…"

"I know where it is," she said, "just find out where this woman is getting her information. Sooner than tomorrow would be good," and Hannah hung up.

Basil tapped his Mont Blanc pen on his desk. How exactly did Hannah think he could find out where Luella was getting her information? Basil called Luella, but she didn't answer.

* * *

Sunningdale

Jonah was up that morning an hour before the sun rose, but he mediated for forty minutes before he picked up *The Times* lying outside his door. When he glanced at the front page, he saw Luella's teaser and he read it, and then he read it again, his eyes tightening in anger.

* * *

London

Luella's cellphone had lit up with over twenty calls from colleagues, relatives, and friends that morning who had read her teaser. When she pulled up the paper online and re-read it, she regretted her dramatic wording. Still, her article would indeed examine an old theory, one that had received little attention at the time of the burglary. Maybe the public would be more interested now in the old crime, which would be good. It deserved renewed attention.

Chapter Nine

Sunningdale

Even though Madeline had gotten little sleep on her flight back to the UK, she blearily jumped into a cab and fell asleep again before she arrived at Sunningdale Golf Club. When she finally got up, she stared at herself in the bathroom mirror for several seconds. Yes, she looked exactly like someone who had just flown over 6,000 miles and back and forth across five time zones in the last thirty-six hours. She wondered what Shay had done while she'd flown to Boston and back. Nothing probably. Madeline unpacked and went for a twenty-minute walk around the grounds of the golf club, calling softly to the gray horses in the paddock. They ignored her. Back in her suite, and after a very long shower and two cups of coffee, Madeline felt a little more awake. She combed through ten estate auction websites, hoping to find an incredible piece for her estate jewelry project, but she didn't find anything. She sent off fifteen more emails to gem dealers, hoping she'd get lucky. She received a reply from only three, but the photos they sent her were of average and overpriced rings. Madeline sent a reply thanking them and left it at that. She needed to take a break from her search for a couple of days.

To take her mind off her failing estate jewelry plan, Madeline went into the closet and sifted through Shay's luggage and then her carry-on bag and took out Shay's laptop. It would be good to take it to her, because it would give Shay something to do, and she left for Heatherwood Hospital.

* * *

At the hospital, she knocked on Shay's door, but there was no answer, so she turned the doorknob and walked in. She was sitting up in her hospital bed, staring at the TV on the wall. The screen was dark.

"You made it back from Boston. You look terrible. There's nothing on TV," said Shay.

"It might help if you turned it on," said Madeline and clicked power button of the TV. A talk show with the host and two smiling guests in black slacks and t-shirts appeared on the screen.

Shay turned away from Madeline, saying in a dull voice, "Turn it off. I'm tired, and I want to sleep. You can go now."

"I have to step out for just a moment," said Madeline, "but I'll be back," and Madeline added, with a smile, "Don't go anywhere."

Shay stared at her with a puzzled frown, and Madeline said, "That was a joke."

Madeline slipped out the door and, at the nurses' station, asked them to page Dr. Marley but was told he was in surgery.

Madeline went back into Shay's room, took Shay's laptop, and set it on the tray table beside her, moving a vase of pink roses.

"I thought you would like to have your computer. I'll charge the battery now."

"Did you bring my other one?" asked Shay.

"What do you mean, your other one?"

"I have two laptops. This one is for work. I brought my personal computer, a mini laptop, with me as well.

"Oh, I didn't see it. I'll bring that one with me tomorrow. Is there anything else I can bring you?" asked Madeline, and opened Shay's work laptop and checked the plug.

Shay shook her head, "Wait, I just changed my mind. Don't bother to bring my mini laptop tomorrow. Just leave it in my luggage." Shay said abruptly, "I can't believe that Kathleen is dead. She was so kind and helpful."

"Yes, you've mentioned that before. It was a tragedy, how awful for her family, and you. Tell me about her, what did Kathleen say that was so helpful?" asked Madeline. "What did the two of you talk about?"

Shay ignored her question and shoved her work laptop aside. "You know what? I don't want my work laptop either. You can take it with you when you leave. I'm too tired to think about anything. I just want to sleep."

"It's only 9:30 in the morning," said Madeline.

Shay just shook her head and stared blankly out the door at the nurses' station, doctors and nurses milling around the desk, talking in low voices.

Shay slid back down in the bed, facing the wall, and pulled the covers up to her neck and finally said, "Chip came by today with Jonah, his boss, who brought me those pink roses, which was so sweet wasn't it? Chip must have told him I like pink and…"

Madeline interrupted, "Yes, I noticed those. They are lovely. By the way, I was surprised that Felix came to pick me up at the airport. He said you called him and told him I was flying into Boston. Why did you do that?"

"I had to because I thought it would be nice if you saw Felix."

"I can't believe that you called him to pick me up at the airport because I…"

Shay interrupted, "Will you really have to sell Coda Gems?"

Tears sprang into Madeline's eyes, and she turned away for a minute, then said over her shoulder, "Yes, we may well have to sell," and she said, changing the subject," Chip told me your photo shoot has been postponed, isn't that great news?"

Shay didn't answer, and a minute later, Madeline realized she had fallen asleep. After ten minutes, Madeline kissed the back of her head and quietly walked out the door. Madeline was worried; Shay only wanted to sleep or stare out the window. It seemed to her that Shay was not getting better, in fact she was getting worse.

* * *

Ascot

Madeline stopped at the nurse's station just as Dr. Marley walked up. He said to her, "I had another MRI run this morning, and the swelling of Mrs. Wolf's brain is receding, which is good news, but I can't release her from the hospital yet. She still has severe nausea, so she must stay in the hospital hooked up to an IV. We can't run the risk of dehydration since it could send her into shock and organ failure."

"I see, so it's good news and bad news?" said Madeline. "I understand why Shay needs to stay in the hospital, but she is still very listless and in a fog. She is not interested in anything, which is not like her at all. Not at all. Should I be concerned?"

"I understand," said Dr. Marley, "I am not concerned, but I am cautious. It will take your sister a little while to get back to normal functioning. What she needs now is rest. It's a little early, to be certain, but she may have post-concussive syndrome. After a concussion, it is not unusual for patients to become very passive and inactive."

"Is there anything I can do?" asked Madeline.

The doctor hesitated and said, "There is a form of cognitive therapy that can possibly help. It would be good if your sister could get involved in a challenging mental activity, something that will require her to think and stay focused. That will help get her brain back on track. However, there does have to be a strong reason for her to start using it because it will require work on her part because of the concussion. She needs a stimulating activity, but it must be one that fully engages her otherwise she won't make the effort. Since you are her sister, you would know better than anyone here what that could be. Sometimes, and it is rare, but her current condition could be long-term, or even permanent."

"Permanent? Permanent? That would be horrible, that would be an absolute catastrophe!" said Madeline. "She is a professional interior photographer, but she is also certified as an Advanced Open Water Scuba Diver and takes photos of whales for non-profits. When can she go back to that?"

Dr. Marley shook his head, "Even though she did not sustain a severe concussion, she absolutely cannot go scuba diving for at least another month because of the possibility of another concussion, which could be deadly. So no, that is out of the question. It would be too dangerous."

"Fine then" said Madeline, running her fingers through her blonde hair. "I'll think about it and come up with an activity for her that that will totally absorb and engage her. Something that is stimulating and challenging but not dangerous, not dangerous at all. How does that sound?"

"That would be very good," said the doctor. "It could make a difference in her recovery. Bear in mind though, board games, or card games or even movies won't be enough, because that is just entertainment. She needs to be mentally challenged by something that is important and meaningful to her. Something that will make her want to concentrate. Let me know what you come up with," he said with a smile, and walked away.

Madeline stared after the doctor; she had no idea where to even start.

* * *

One of Shay's nurses walked past, and Madeline stopped her. "You have my sister's purse, don't you? You must have it since her passport would have been in her purse. Her passport should stay with her, but I should probably take her purse with me."

The nurse went out the door, and came back with Shay's purse, as well as a heavy canvas bag with an outline of the UK studded in red, Swarovski crystals. She set on the floor, and nodded to the bag, "Do you know who this belongs to?"

"No, I've never seen that before. Where did it come from?"

"It was in Kathleen's car," said the nurse, "One of the EMTs at the accident said it was on your sister's lap when they arrived at the scene, so we assumed it was hers. It was very lucky she was holding it. When the tow truck struck the car, a heavy chunk of the dashboard was torn off and slammed into the passenger seat where she was sitting."

The nurse showed Madeline a long, jagged gash in the bag and said, "If

102

your sister hadn't had it in her lap, that chunk of dashboard would have hit her directly in the chest, which could have killed her. But it hit this heavy canvas bag first, so she ended up only very bruised."

Madeline ran her fingers over a wide, ragged hole in the center of the bag and carefully opened it. Inside were stacked copies of newspaper and magazine articles.

"Oh yes, Shay mentioned this," said Madeline, "she told me that Kathleen, she was the woman driving the car, gave it to her."

"Then you should definitely take this with you, too," said the nurse.

"Well, alright then, I will," said Madeline. "Please tell Shay I'll be back tomorrow morning."

Madeline slung Shay's purse over her shoulder and lugged the canvas bag to the front door of the hospital. As she waited outside for the car from the club to arrive, tears suddenly welled up her eyes, and she had to brush them away. Madeline was worried, afraid that her sweet and injured sister would permanently disappear into a confused fog of indifference.

A minute later, the car arrived, and Madeline wiped away the last of her tears and lifted the canvas bag into the back seat of the car, getting in beside it.

* * *

Sunningdale

Back in her room at the club, Madeline made a cup of tea, although what she really needed was a cup of strong, bullet-proof coffee, and she opened the canvas bag. She glanced through the top stories; fewer than ten had been published in the last ten years. She dug deeper and found a smattering of stories every year starting in the 80s, and even into the late 90s, and then maybe one story each year after. The majority of the stories were older, most of them from the 1930s and 40s. She shoved the bag in a closet.

She'd keep the canvas bag itself of course since it had saved Shay's life, but she'd tell her tomorrow she had Kathleen's big bag of news articles, and they should be thrown away. It made no sense to hold onto them.

Madeline walked into the bedroom, and searched through Shay's suitcase in the closet again, this time looking for her mini laptop. She pulled out several pair of jeans and sweatshirts. Shay's underwear was, no surprise, pink, and expensive; at least they didn't have red hearts embroidered on them. In the closet was a beige suit, four blouses on hangers, and a pair of low brown heels. She didn't find a small laptop.

Madeline took out Shay's carry-on and in a hidden compartment in the back Madeline found her small laptop and set it on the desk. Shay had told her not to bring it to the hospital, but Madeline took it to a small desk and chair off the living room. She didn't give a second thought about prying, because that's what sisters do.

She plugged it in, and a sign-in screen popped up. Years ago, Shay mentioned that she always used Shay Ann as her ID and Harrison Heart46 as the password for all her devices, so Madeline typed in that information.

Shay's computer screen lit up, and over twenty folders appeared. All the folders were named for different species of whales, except one folder titled "Sunningdale." Madeline clicked that one open.

Two PDFs were inside; the first one was a copy of a faded newspaper article dated Oct. 17, 1946.

Duchess of Windsor Jewels Stolen in Sunningdale

"The Duke and Duchess of Windsor, weekend guests of the Earl and Countess of Dudley, were victims of a theft at Ednam Lodge, the Earl's country estate in Sunningdale on Tuesday evening, Oct. 16th. The celebrated couple was dining in London when the burglary occurred.

The Duchess' jewelry case was stolen, which included a 41-cart sapphire ring, a 58-carat aquamarine solitaire, and a 25-carat diamond and platinum necklace. Also stolen was an eight-carat Burmese ruby ring in a platinum setting, along with a number of other rings and bracelets. The Duchess had recently purchased a 'Bird of Paradise' brooch, with 20 carats of rubies, a large cabochon sapphire, and over 12 carats of *diamonds that is also missing.*

Unfortunately, the morning of the theft the Earl's staff had offered to store the Duchess' leather bag of jewels in the earl's safe, but she had declined. Instead, according to the maid, the Duchess slid the jewelry case under the bed in their upstairs bedroom.

R.M. Howe, Assistant Commissioner of Scotland Yard, has been placed in charge of the investigation with over a dozen detectives assigned to the case full-time. A reward has been offered by Scotland Yard for information leading to the recovery of the jewels."

Madeline opened the second PDF titled "The Stolen Pieces." It was a one-page list of the twenty pieces of the Duchess' jewelry that had been stolen from the earl's home. According to the date stamp on the document, Shay must have typed this the afternoon of the car accident, right before she left to meet with Kathleen.

The first piece of jewelry on Shay's list was the Duchess' Burmese ruby ring, which Shay had typed in all caps, a string of exclamation marks after it. Madeline sighed; her sister was still obsessed with the Duchess's stolen eight-carat ruby ring. Shay couldn't seem to get it off her mind.

At that moment, Madeline had a sudden idea, a knock-down, drop-dead brilliant idea, and she laughed out loud. She had just found the perfect 'brain exercise' for Shay.

Dr. Marley had said Shay needed to work her brain and get it back on track by becoming fully engaged in a challenge that was important and meaningful to her. Madeline knew she had just found the perfect challenge.

She would ask her sister to help her figure out who had stolen the Duchess's jewels eighty years ago, and the way for the two of them to do that was to read as much as possible about the crime and then talk to people in Sunningdale who might have information. The best part was that Kathleen's bag of news articles had pages and pages of reading material. All Shay would have to do would be to get Shay to start reading the articles, which would require her to concentrate, which was *exactly* what the doctor had ordered.

To be honest, Madeline would rather stick needles in her eyes than delve into the old, boring jewelry crime, whether a burglary or an insurance scam; either way, it was a crime. But Madeline would focus on the theft possibility because that would be more intriguing to Shay. Madeline knew getting her to help try and figure out who had 'stolen' the jewelry was not just a good plan; it was a brilliant one. Madeline was positive that Shay would jump at the chance to figure out who had stolen the Duchess' jewelry, and it was the absolute perfect exercise to get her to concentrate and use her brain. As an added plus, it was not at all dangerous.

But first, Madeline had to make Shay believe she was serious about delving into the mystery of the lost jewelry. She'd already told Shay more than once that she believed the crime had been nothing more than a boring insurance scam, but she changed her mind.

Madeline went through Kathleen's most recent news articles, and for twenty minutes she scanned the news stories from the least ten years that rehashed the details of the missing jewelry. All of them treated it as a burglary, so Madeline would too, because it was a more intriguing riddle for Shay than insurance fraud. However, Madeline knew she would have to be enthusiastic when she talked to Shay, and Madeline knew she would be enthusiastic, just not for the reason Shay would think.

Madeline gritted her teeth; there was not a single thing she found interesting about the missing jewelry, except for the ex-king-emperor part. She looked at her cell phone, it was only 4:00 in the afternoon. Madeline called the front desk and asked for a ride to Heatherwood Hospital. She wanted to talk to Shay about her brilliant plan and get Shay to work her brain right away. There was no time to waste.

Madeline dropped fifty news articles from the late 1940s in a leather bag and went outside to wait for the car and driver.

* * *

Ascot

At the hospital, the door to Shay's room was half open. Madeline knocked once and walked in, the leather bag in her hand. Shay was sitting up in bed, staring blankly out the window. She turned when Madeline came in and set the bag on Shay's bed.

"Jonah was here again," said Shay. "He stopped in this afternoon to see how I was doing. He said he just got back from wherever he was, I forget where. He is good looking, in a swashbuckling kind of way. I like him."

"I've never met Jonah," said Madeline, "but he seems very concerned about you, and it is very generous of him to give me a room as well as a car and driver to visit you."

"Yes," said Shay, "he has been great, and I think he…" She stopped and pointed to the leather bag on her bed. "What is that?"

"This," said Madeline as she picked up the bag, "has to do with a great idea."

"A great idea?" said Shay. "Have you come to smuggle me out of here?"

"Soon, you'll be leaving here soon. I came to tell you about my plan, a fabulous plan about the Duchess of Windsor's jewels,"

"What about them?"

"When I left here this morning," said Madeline, "a nurse gave me a big canvas bag of old news articles about her missing jewelry that Kathleen had copied for you, so I took it back to the Club."

"I forgot about Kathleen's canvas bag. I'm glad you have it because Kathleen said it was important."

"I took a good look at some of her older newspaper articles," said Madeline, "as well as a couple more recent ones. And guess what, Shay, I've totally changed my mind about that whole story. I know I told you it was tedious and boring and that I…"

"What you said was that you were sick to death of it," Shay pointed out.

"I said that?"

"Yes. You said that more than once. You were quite definite, too. You also said it was an insurance…what do you call it…scam." Shay turned back to the window, staring at the sidewalk out front.

"Well, I'm not sick of it anymore," said Madeline. "I've done a bit of reading, and now it makes me want to find out what really happened that day right here in Sunningdale," said Madeline, and she knew she sounded genuinely enthusiastic, because she was. "And Shay, I know you'll love my idea, because I am now convinced the disappearance of the jewelry was indeed a burglary, and I have an idea."

Shay turned and looked at Madeline, "You are convinced now it was a burglary? What is your idea?"

"So here we are, the two of us," began Madeline, "close to the scene of a very famous burglary that was never solved. The big mystery is, who stole the Duchess's jewelry? We should try and figure out who that person could possibly be."

Shay sat up in her hospital bed, her eyes glued on Madeline.

"I think we," said Madeline, "should try and figure that out, or narrow it down, to who was the most likely thief. God knows because of Kathleen we have nearly everything that has been written about it. We can at least come up with some good guesses, since any proof is long gone. We can take a hard look at the facts and see what we can uncover, and maybe, with any luck, come up with the truth. We won't look for the jewels because God knows where they are. We'll just concentrate on identifying the thief. Nobody has ever gotten close to doing that before."

"You want to identify the thief? Really?"

"Yes, but I need a partner to help, and you would be perfect because you're already up to speed on the Duchess' jewelry. I think you and I should follow the clues and see what we can figure out."

Shay looked at Madeline, "Are you serious? You're not serious, are you?

Madeline nodded, "I am serious. I think together we should go through the old information Kathleen gave you, because two heads are better than one. We will be 'amateur sleuths' and check around and see what we can dig up here, in Sunningdale. I love that term, amateur sleuth, don't you? Isn't it just perfect? And Jonah is important since it happened next door to his golf club. He should be the first person we should talk to since he has probably heard a lot of stories about it over the years. I am positive he has helpful information."

"That makes sense," said Shay slowly, "Jonah will be critical."

"Yes, he will be. With any luck he could also give us recommendations for other people we should talk to as well, which would be great," said Madeline.

"You've changed your mind," said Shay, slowly, her eyebrows furrowed in concentration, "You did say, at least once, that even thinking about it would be a waste of time, didn't you? But I don't understand why now, all if a sudden, that you don't think that anymore and that you want to…" Shay paused, searching for a word, and finally came up with it, "investigate."

"Yes, I did think that it was a waste of time, but that was before I read some of the old newspaper reports, and I've changed my mind," lied Madeline quite smoothly, she thought. "In my opinion, the whole thing needs to be reexamined carefully. The beauty of amateur sleuths is they can sometimes see things that the professionals missed, things that the professionals overlooked."

Madeline thought that was a great line. She had no idea if it was true or not, but it sounded like it might be true.

"Amateur sleuths," repeated Shay slowly, she said with a big smile. "I like it, I like it a lot. Yes, we should do this. I've already read a lot about her stolen jewelry."

This was the first time Madeline had seen Shay really smile since she'd arrived in the UK. "So, you'll be my partner then?" said Madeline.

"Yes, of course, we need to find out who stole 'my' ruby ring." Then she held up her right arm with the IV tube hanging down. "But what about this?"

"Don't worry about that. For now, I'll do the running around and the 'talking to people part'. I have stacks and stacks of copies of Kathleen's newspaper reports going back to 1946 for you to start reading."

Shay laughed, "That sounds perfect!"

Madeline nodded to the leather bag on Shay's bed, "Great. I brought old newspaper reports from the 1940s for you to start with. The rest are in a big canvas bag back at the club, and I'll bring all of them to you tomorrow, and then we'll come up with what we need to do next, and we'll talk to people, starting with Jonah of course."

"Maybe we'll even find the Duchess' jewels," said Shay. "Wouldn't that be amazing?"

Madeline hesitated, because finding the jewelry was well beyond a 'when pigs fly' possibility, so she said, "I think we should just focus on the day of the burglary, and then the next day. Who was there at the scene of the crime, why were they there, and what did they do once the theft was discovered."

Shay sat up in her hospital bed, her legs dangling over the edge of the bed, speaking quickly, her eyes narrowed again, "But Madeline, I am surprised you are interested in this, because you..."

Madeline shrugged, "Well, I am now very interested, especially since we're right here, right where the burglary happened. We'll go through the articles together and come up with a plan. A good plan."

"When you come here tomorrow,w can you bring my mini laptop plus my Nikon camera that's in my luggage? You never know. We might need a camera," she laughed. "In books, amateur sleuths always have cameras. My work cameras, as well as my lenses and equipment, aren't in my suite. I had them shipped here a week ago, and they're in a locked security room at the club, but my trusty Nikon should be just fine, for now."

"Of course." Madeline looked at her watch, "I should be going, I need to organize Kathleen's pages and go through all of them again, before I bring them to you tomorrow."

Madeline reached into the leather bag, took out the fifty pages of newspaper reports, and handed them to Shay. "You can start reading these this afternoon, don't worry, some of them are pretty short. Do read them carefully, though, and make notes and write down any questions you think are important. Tonight, I'll come up with a summary of what we know and initial questions we have, and I'll bring that with me when I come to see you tomorrow morning. How about I come by at 8:30 am?"

"Perfect," said Shay. "I will start reading as soon as you leave. Who knows what we will come up with."

Madeline leaned over and hugged Shay, "Just be sure to pay close attention to what you're reading, and then write down your thoughts," said Madeline. Her cell phone rang, and she glanced down. It was Abby. She'd call her back later.

Madeline was not about to tell Abby what she and Shay were up to. Abby would approve of the 'helping Shay' part, but she wouldn't be crazy about Madeline getting even marginally involved in checking into an old burglary. Abby would say to her, with just a bit of sarcasm because she wouldn't be able to help it, "Who do you think you are, Nancy Drew?" Abby had said that to Madeline before, several times, which never failed to irritate her.

Madeline did know it would be a bad idea to mention any of this to Felix because he'd just tell her she was out of her mind to be mixed up in anything criminal, even if the criminals were long dead. She also suspected Felix would have opinions, and she didn't have the time, or the interest, to deal with him.

At the door, Madeline waved goodbye to Shay, surprised as well as relieved that she could already see even just a hint of change in Shay's affect. The only thing that mattered now was that Shay continued to believe they were conducting a real investigation. Which meant Madeline needed to learn more about the robbery.

* * *

Sunningdale

On Madeline's way back to the golf club, she had the driver stop at a grocery store. She picked up a big bag of coffee with a powerful name, "Death Wish Coffee." She needed something strong, something to keep her interested as she plowed through stacks of dull reports of a story that had put her teeth on edge for years.

* * *

The first thing Madeline did after she walked in the door of the suite was to make a pot of "Death Wish Coffee" which was as strong as advertised, it was sledge-hammer strong. After she finished her coffee, she dragged Kathleen's canvas bag from the closet to the dining room and set the formidable stacks of articles on the small table, dividing them by decade.

For seven hours that afternoon and evening Madeline sat at a small desk off her bedroom, reading. Two pots of Death Wish helped as she skimmed every article published in the UK that was in Kathleen's canvas bag.

For years, Madeline had dismissed the robbery as a simple case of insurance fraud that had been 'ginned up" by the media into a fascinating and mysterious burglary. But after the third hour, she changed her mind. It had been a burglary and a complicated one. It had also not been a burglary of simple luck. To pull it off, the thief or thieves had to know what they were looking for and where to find it. Still, since there had been an actual burglary, why hadn't the police ever come close to solving it. Why not?

Because maybe, for whatever reason, they didn't want to identify the thief?

After four hours of reading the news reports, Madeline needed to call Abby for their daily Coda Gems call, and as their call was ending, Madeline mentioned the background materials she'd been reading on the case.

"I've never had an opportunity to quote from 'Alice in Wonderland' before," she'd said to Abby, "but I am finding the whole Duchess of Windsor's burglary 'curiouser and curiouser.' Almost all the specifics I've read about the disappearance of the jewels are unlikely, even improbable. It was a miracle the burglary was even pulled off."

"Maybe you should just stop reading about it then," said Abby, "especially if it's, as you have said, a waste of time. So, you don't think it was just an insurance scam?"

"No, but that doesn't matter. All I want is for Shay to be totally engaged, because it will be fun for the two of us to talk about. In my opinion, the caper had been well planned by criminal minds, except for the ending."

"What do you mean?" asked Abby.

"The collection of jewelry vanished and stayed that way, so I think something unexpected happened at the end," said Madeline.

After she hung up with Abby, she pulled off the next news report from the closest stack, this one just a single page. It was just a snippet of what must have been a longer article, only a couple of sentences, which mentioned an award of the Royal Victorian Order. Someone had scrawled a question mark and the word 'Why?' in black ink and had underlined it. Interesting.

Madeline googled the award, an honor handed out by the reigning British monarch for 'distinguished personal service to the monarch. 'The word 'Why?' was a curious comment, and she read it again and slid it into her briefcase because it seemed odd and then forgot about it.

She plowed through the rest of the stacks of Kathleen's copies until she finished.

Madeline knew the theft was mysterious: no clues, no real suspects, and no jewels. Nothing about the crime made any sense because it shouldn't have worked, yet it did, and the investigation didn't make any sense either because no real suspects were ever identified even after the investigation had dragged on and eventually ground to a halt after fifteen years. R.M. Howe, Assistant Commissioner of Scotland Yard, has been placed in charge of the burglary investigation, with a dozen detectives assigned to the case full-time. Was it odd that such a very high-ranking officer had been put in charge of what was basically just a jewelry theft and one that was never solved?

Madeline knew she had to make sure their "investigation" seemed as real as possible, or Shay would not take it seriously. For the next hour, Madeline put together an overview of the key elements from the day of the jewelry and challenging questions that she and Shay should try and answer. Once Madeline was satisfied, she printed off her two-page overview laying out the facts.

OVERVIEW: ASSUMPTIONS AND QUESTIONS
The Scene of the Crime: The Second Home of the Earl of Dudley
On-Site Security: Two Scotland Yard Bodyguards

Assumption: The thief had to have had information from a source inside the earl's home. The burglary was not a robbery of convenience but had to have been based on inside information: The afternoon of the theft, in broad daylight, the thief had apparently climbed up a drainpipe next to the Windsors' bedroom window on the second floor, crawled in, and likely left with the Duchess' case of jewels the same way.

1. Location of the Jewelry: The thief knew which bedroom on the second floor of the house was the Windsors'. Also, the thief apparently knew the Duchess' jewelry was in a gray custom-made titanium case. How did the thief know to look for that?

2. Lack of Security: The case of jewelry had not been locked up in one of the earl's two safes in his house. Instead, the Duchess had simply tucked the case of jewelry under the bed in her and the duke's bedroom. It also seemed the thief knew where to find the case, since it did not appear that the burglar had rummaged through the closets, nor dresser drawers looking for it. Instead, the thief apparently knew the case of jewelry was under the bed.

3. Geography: Someone would have had to tell the thief which window on the second floor was the window in the Windsor's bedroom.

4. Absence of the Windsors: Someone had to have let the thief know the Windsors would leave the earl's home the afternoon of the burglary for dinner in London, since the thief was seemingly not concerned the couple might unexpectedly walk into their bedroom when he came through the bedroom window.

Timing: It seemed that the burglary likely happened during the servants' tea-time, when they would have all been in the servants' lounge between 3:00 and 4:00, which was on the other side of the house from the Windsors' bedroom.

1. Professionalism: On the face of it, the theft seemed amateurish and a matter of lucky happenstance, or maybe that was on purpose, to make it look like the theft had been a simple crime of opportunity. Yet someone had closely coordinated the theft. Who?

Questions:

A. Could a friend or acquaintance of one of the servants have pulled off the theft?

B. Could the Scotland bodyguards have masterminded and then conducted the theft?

C. How could a dozen Scotland Yard detectives have failed to identify the thief even with MI5's involvement? It was an open investigation for fifteen years, yet no viable suspect was ever charged by police.

D. Not a single piece of jewelry was ever recovered except for Queen Mary's pearl necklace that the thief had apparently dropped on the greens of the Sunningdale Golf Course. Why such a sloppy escape? As important, why didn't the thief have a getaway car?

E. What happened with the case of jewelry after the burglar had taken it?

F. Was the jewelry still in Sunningdale, hidden away by the thief, or had it been smuggled out of the UK?

Madeline was pleased with her two-page overview and made several copies.

Madeline knew that Shay would pay close attention to the pages she'd left with her the day before to read, but would probably have to struggle with them, which was perfect. It would force Shay to use her brain to follow the ins and outs of the burglary and help her brain recover.

Madeline smiled. She loved her plan.

Chapter Ten

London

L uella had taken the train into London for drinks and a late dinner that evening at The Red Apple near Pimlico Station with a fellow reporter from *The Telegraph*.

"You saw the teaser for my feature article in the paper today? said Luella as the two women were shown to a table in the back with faded leather chairs. Above the low hum of the diners was the faint sounds of Miles Davis's 'Bitches Brew'.

"Of course, I saw it," said Luella's friend as the two ordered dinner and a round of drinks. "The teaser was hard to miss since it was on the front page. Did you write it, or did your editor?"

"I wrote it. My editor hasn't seen my article because I haven't finished it yet. It's close, but not quite ready. He called me, panicked, and told me I had to come up with a teaser for him. He said he needed it right away or I might lose the space for my article next week, so guess what, I wrote it right away."

"When will the article itself run?"

"Next Wednesday," said Luella. "My editor just texted me that it will run a day earlier than originally planned, because there apparently has been a lot of interest stirred up by my teaser. My article is relatively long, about two thousand words, and it ends with an explosive conjecture." She laughed, "It doesn't provide any answers about that old theft, but it will raise some very important questions in the minds of the readers."

"About what?"

"About collusion," said Luella, and she smiled. "That all I can say, for now."

* * *

After a long dinner and two more scotch and sodas, one a double, Luella left her friend at the restaurant and made her way to the train station to head back to Sunningdale. One of the London Underground's ubiquitous CCTV cameras had captured her that evening standing on the platform at Pimlico, watching the slowing train to Sunningdale approach the platform. At 11:43 pm Luella walked toward the edge of the platform, and when the train to come to a stop, she boarded.

However, she did not disembark at the Sunningdale station stop, nor did she get off at any of the other stations further down the line. Luella never walked off the train.

Instead, Luella's body was found at 3:25 am by a station worker along the tracks two miles from the Bracknell stop. The immediate and official cause of death was blunt force trauma, the result of an accidental fall from an unattended door on a speeding train. Train procedures for securing exits were immediately strengthened across all train lines.

* * *

The next morning *The Times* ran a short announcement of Luella's accidental death on the newspaper's front page, with full details on page five. Luella's editor Christopher had written a florid tribute.

* * *

As usual, Basil scanned front page of *The Times* over his usual early morning breakfast at his flat in Fulham but stopped cold when he read the announcement of Luella's death, and he set his plate of scrambled eggs to the side. He turned to page five and read the sketchy details of Luella's fall from a train traveling at seventy miles an hour. He called Hannah.

"Have you read *The Times*? Did you read about that reporter, Luella Kloberdanz?"

"Yes. I saw the announcement, so she is dead. It appears to have been an accident."

"It's hard to believe," said Basil uneasily.

"It does seem strange," said Hannah, "but then accidents do happen. I am guessing she had probably been drinking. It's all very sad," and she hung up.

Chapter Eleven

Ascot

At 8:30 a.m., Madeline walked into Shay's hospital room carrying Kathleen's canvas bag with the rest of Kathleen's articles, and she set it on the floor. Shay was sitting up in her bed, smiling, the fifty pages Madeline had left her the day before scattered across the coverlet. Several sheets of lined paper that were filled with Shay's elegant handwriting lay on the bedside table.

"How did your reading go yesterday?" said Madeline and sat in a chair by Shay's bed.

"I didn't go to bed until almost 1:30 am," said Shay, yawning. "It took me a long time to read everything. To be honest, it was hard in the beginning, and I had to read the first fifteen pages five or six times, but I got through them, and then I somehow managed to read the rest, every page, and after that, I made notes. It was difficult, but I loved doing it."

One of the hospital's doctors walked past Shay's door and stuck his head in the door, "Good morning, Mrs. Wolf," and he gave her a big smile. Madeline laughed when Shay's return smile was equally brilliant, a definite sign she was on the mend.

"That's great that you read everything," said Madeline, "good job," and she pointed to Kathleen's bag. "I brought a lot more articles for you to read, a lot more, but they will give you an even better picture of the investigation. Some of the articles are very old, but I thought you'd like to read everything that was available. You don't need to read all of them, maybe just another ninety or one hundred newspaper reports."

Madeline looked at the pages spread on the bed, "It's great that you made notes of what you read last night. I'll take them with me when I leave, and we can talk about it tomorrow, if you're interested."

Shay leaned over and peered into the bag, "Of course I'm interested, how could I not be interested? I'll start reading the next pages as soon as you leave."

Madeline handed Shay her two-page Overview: Assumptions and Questions, and Shay began to read it.

"I thought," said Madeline, "that a good place for us to start would be to go over my Overview this morning. Are you up for that?"

Shay didn't reply but concentrated on reading the two pages."Yes, of course, and you are right," she finally replied, glancing up from Madeline's overview. "You are definitely correct. The burglar had to have inside information."

"Yes, he did, but how did the burglar get it? Let's talk about the potential sources for us to talk to," said Madeline. "Of course, the first person we need to talk to is Jonah. We shouldn't tell him that we're looking to identify the burglar. We'll just tell him that we're trying to get a sense of what happened that night because we're fascinated by the Duchess's jewelry. That should be enough."

"Why say that? Is it because trying to identify the burglar sounds weird?" Shay said.

"Yes, because you know what, Shay, it is weird. Two American sisters nosing around Sunningdale trying to identify the thief in a very old and very famous British burglary is a bit strange."

A nurse stuck her head in the door and said to Madeline, "Dr. Marley thought he saw you walking down the hall, and he would like to speak to you for a moment."

"Of course," said Madeline, and to Shay, she said, "I'll be right back."

* * *

Madeline followed the nurse out the door. However, the doctor had been pulled into an emergency consult, and he couldn't be interrupted. Five minutes later, when she walked back into Shay's room, a tall, burly man in his late 50s, in black jeans and a *Doctors Without Borders* sweatshirt, was sitting in the chair by Shay's bed. He had Kathleen's bag of magazine and newspaper articles on the floor by his chair, and he was reading Madeline's two-page overview. The morning's edition of *The Times of London,* apparently his, lay open on Shay's bed. Jonah was frowning when he looked up at Madeline, his eyes a hard, unsmiling gray. He glanced at the front page again as he stood up.

Shay said, "Jonah, this is my sister, Madeline Lane."

"Jonah Musgrave," he said, stepping forward, and he and Madeline shook hands. His handshake was firm, his hand callused; the man worked outdoors. He watched Madeline carefully, not taking his eyes off her.

"I am glad to meet you," said Madeline and pulled up a chair, "thank you for making one of your beautiful suites available for me, as well as a car service to go back and forth to see Shay. You have made a challenging time a lot easier for me and my sister."

"I am happy to do it," he said. "Shay's accident was horrible." He looked at Shay and then turned to Madeline, "I understand the two of you are 'fascinated' with the theft of the Duchess of Windsor's jewelry, or words to that effect," he said, his voice now abruptly cold.

Shay stopped flipping through a pile of newspaper reports on her bed, watching Jonah.

"Why are you so interested?" he said bluntly to Madeline. "What are you up to?"

"Well," began Madeline carefully, "Shay and I are intrigued by the story of the theft, and of course, the Duchess of Windsor did have an incredible jewelry collection. Shay may have mentioned I am in the jewelry business. We are hoping to get your help. It would be great if you could tell us what you remember hearing about the burglary from your father. That way, we can have a better understanding of what..."

"I won't help you with your...fascination or investigation, or whatever you want to call it," said Jonah. "The burglary was a long time ago, and I want NO part of raking through it all over again. I can't help you."

"No? We were looking forward to your feedback…do you really mean we can't talk to you about it?"

"Correct. My father was obsessed with the theft, and he even dug up a couple of fairways looking for the jewelry. He didn't find anything, but he still talked about it, making new plans, and then he backed off." Jonah sighed and looked at Madeline.

"He just…backed off? Do you know why?" asked Madeline.

"No, I did ask him, more than once, and he would only say, 'Let sleeping dogs lie.'"

"So, we can't even…" persisted Madeline.

Jonah shook his head no and stood up, "I have a call in five minutes. Don't become too preoccupied with the Duchess' jewelry. It could be dangerous. Sorry."

Jonah didn't look sorry.

He kissed Shay on the cheek, shook Madeline's hand again, and walked out of the hospital room. Jonah had left his copy of the *Times* on the bed, and Madeline picked it up and went out the door after him, but he had already walked down the hall and out the door. She jammed his newspaper in her briefcase. She'd give it to him later. If she felt like it.

"I wonder what that was all about?" said Shay said to Madeline as she gathered the strewn copies of news reports in a pile on the bed.

Madeline sighed, "Well, I did not expect him to say he wouldn't help us, and he was quite definite about that. As far as his warning about danger, he could just be the dramatic type," and Madeline straightened her shoulders. "Now that he is out of the picture, we will just have to work on our plan without him."

"Without Jonah? How do we do that?"

"We'll just have to find other people to talk to on our own," said Madeline, "How long has Chip been working here? I can ask him for help in identifying people in Sunningdale who might have information."

"Chip has been working here for almost a year," said Shay, "but I can't ask

122

him for any names since it would get back to Jonah, and Jonah wouldn't like it. Will you ask Felix what he thinks? He does investigate crimes for a living."

"I will certainly not ask Felix. He knows nothing about what's been going on, and he's already consumed by his North Sea Oil story. Besides, l already know what he'll say, since he's said it to me about a thousand times, 'I always talk to the police first if there's been a crime since they have at least some information, then I check out the local news, and after that I talk to my sources.'"

"Felix would be very pleased you remembered," said Shay.

"I am not about to mention it to him," said Madeline, "his ego is already inflated enough as it is. Felix thinks he is God's gift to…well, everyone."

Out of the corner of her eye, Madeline saw Dr. Marley beckon to her from the corridor, and she said to Shay, "Hold on a minute, I'll be back." She went out to the corridor and spoke with him.

Five minutes later, she walked back in.

"Did you just call Felix?" asked Shay.

"I did not. I talked to your doctor. He said your nausea is under control, and you can be off the IV this afternoon or tomorrow, and you can be released from the hospital in…

"I know, Dr. Marley already told me that, but what I want to know is when and how do we start figuring out who stole the Duchess's jewelry now that Jonah won't help? We do need to get working on this right away, especially since we'll be leaving Sunningdale soon. So, what do we do next, what should we focus on, but most important, when do we start?"

"Start?" said Madeline. She hadn't expected Shay to be so enthusiastic, and after a pause, said, "Well, let's start right now and think about the day of the crime. Who had access to specific information about the duke and duchess's stay with the Earl of Dudley, and of those who did, who could come and go in the house with no one paying particular attention? The answer is the bodyguards. They would have known everything that was going on at Ednam Lodge, so we should start with the bodyguards. It could be that they either stole the jewelry or know who did. Everything points to them."

"I think you could be right, but they've been dead for a long time."

"True, but we can still find out what they did and where they were that night. It would be great if we could get our hands on a copy of the police report since they certainly talked to the bodyguards." Madeline thought for a moment, "Since Felix said he always begins with the police, that's what we should do. I'll go and have a chat with the chief of police or whatever he or she is called in Sunningdale next. Why don't you come up with a couple of questions you think I should ask the police? After all, the bodyguards would have had to have been suspects at the time.

"Once I have that information," continued Madeline, "I'll go to a library and read up on any other news that was published in Sunningdale right around the day of the burglary, which will give us a good idea of what was happening. Finally, when we're finished, we'll come up with a list of possible sources to talk to."

"I am sure the bodyguards were interviewed," said Shay.

"Yes, that would have been automatic," said Madeline and dropped a notepad in her purse. "I'd like to talk to the police today, so could you give me about four questions you think I should ask them? Read a couple more articles if you think it will help."

"No problem," said Shay, "but give me a couple of minutes, and I'll do it right now, since I've read so much about the burglary already," and she sifted through the stacks of newspaper reports and started writing. "The first question should be, what are their names."

Ten minutes later, Shay read four questions out loud to Madeline.

Shay' speech was still a little slow, but the difference in her thinking was noticeable. Her questions were succinct, and relevant; What were the bodyguards' names? Anything unusual in their Scotland Yard employment record, or problems like alcohol or gambling? What were their actions before and right after the burglary? The last one was a request for a copy of the police report from the night of the burglary.

"Terrific," said Madeline, "you did a really, really good job, and you've come up with some great ones. I really like your third question, 'What were the bodyguards' actions right before and right after the burglary.' I'll have to ask that carefully, though, since I don't want the cops to believe we suspect the bodyguards were involved in the theft since they might ask a lot of questions."

"Sounds good," said Shay, "When do we leave?"

Madeline ignored the question, "First, I need to do some background research since I need a plausible story for showing up and asking questions about the bodyguards. I have an idea, but I need to work on it for fifteen minutes or so."

Madeline searched on her cell phone for the closest Royal Air Force base to Sunningdale, saying to Shay over her shoulder, "I need a local connection to Sunningdale, and then I'll add in a little WWII red herring because people in law enforcement love war stories."

"Shay, I would have you come with me to the police station, but you would be a distraction. Your bruises are now a lovely color, but they would require an explanation. You know how cops are," said Madeline.

She pulled a pen and notebook from her purse and wrote furiously, and after fifteen minutes, she announced she had her story ready for the police and told Shay she'd be back soon. Madeline went outside and grabbed a cab in front of the hospital for the Sunningdale Police Station, which was quicker than waiting for a car from the club.

Chapter Twelve

Sunningdale

Once inside the police station, Madeline said to the officer at the front desk, "My name is Madeline Lane, and I am from Boston, in the US. My grandfather was assigned to the High Wycombe Air Force Base here in the UK from 1944-1946, and I have a few questions for the chief of police if he or she is available."

"She is called the chief constable," said the officer.

Madeline smiled, but she was uneasy and looked around. She hoped she wouldn't see Detective Buckingham and need to launch into a phony explanation of why she was at the police station.

Five minutes later, the heavy-set chief constable of Sunningdale walked out to the small waiting area. The woman was not happy, "I was told you have a couple of questions, something about the RAF High Wycombe Air Force Base?" she said, eyeing Madeline with suspicion, "You're American, right? Why are you here? Why don't you just go to the base and ask them your questions? It's not that far away you know. Google it, and get their address," she ended, not hiding her annoyance.

"It's complicated. Yes, I am an American. My name is Madeline Lane. I'm here visiting my sister at Heatherwood Hospital," and she began her story, "I am writing a family history, and my grandfather, Jasper Lane, was temporarily assigned to the RAF base over at High Wycombe from 1943-1945 by the US Army.

"The Duke and Duchess of Windsor had two bodyguards with them when they were in Sunningdale in Oct. of 1946, and my grandfather knew one of the bodyguards from the war, and they met for lunch while the bodyguard was on duty here. I don't remember the bodyguard's name, but my grandfather told me their lunch lasted for two hours. At the end, the bodyguard gave my grandfather one of his medals from the war, and I always wondered what the story was behind it. The medal meant something important to both of them, because my grandfather hung it in a place of honor in his living room for thirty years. I am guessing my father trained him to fly bombers during the war. My family would love it if I could include that information, including the man's name, in my family history."

"Your American grandfather was a pilot with the RAF?"

"No, he was sent here during the war as an instructor on B-17s."

"Really?" and the constable and smiled. "My grandfather was a pilot, but I don't think I ever knew what he flew. How can I help you?"

"I am hoping to learn the bodyguards' names and any other information you might have on them." said Madeline, "so I can look up their war records in London before I fly back to Boston. My grandfather did tell me the bodyguard's name a long time ago, but I don't remember it."

"Do you have the medal with you?"

"No, it's in Boston. I flew to London very suddenly because my sister was injured in a car accident in Ascot."

"Where are you staying?" asked the constable.

"The Sunningdale Golf Club."

The constable smiled and glanced at the clock on the wall, "I see, well come with me to my office, and I'll try and find some information for you."

"Thank you. I appreciate anything you can do."

＊＊＊

Madeline followed her to a small office, with tall stacks of papers on a battered desk and several smaller stacks on the floor. The woman clicked on a computer, and Madeline took a pen and a notepad from her bag.

After ten minutes of searching, the constable pulled up a couple of folders on her desktop and opened the last one. And after two minutes, she said, "Here it is, the bodyguards that weekend were with Scotland Yard, and their names were Leonard Johanns and Dick Meirick." The constable slowly spelled their names for Madeline.

"Thanks so much. Both of the names sound familiar," said Madeline, "but I'm not quite sure which one my grandfather knew," lied Madeline smoothly, writing down their names. Do you have any other information?" she asked. "Anything unusual in their service records, like any problems, such as gambling or alcohol?"

The constable stared at her, and Madeline laughed, "My grandfather loved gossip so that might help jog my memory of what he told me. Anyway, what did the bodyguards do right before or right after the theft? That might be helpful, too."

The constable quickly glanced through three of the folders on her desktop. After five minutes, she said, "Both bodyguards were just ordinary mid-level officers, nothing unusual at all in their service records, nothing at all. As far as what they did right before the burglary, Officer Johanns left Ednam Lodge on an 'unexpected errand' at 3:00 for Holy Trinity, something about..." and the constable squinted and looked up, "The entry was handwritten, and I can't make it out. Anyway, Officer Johanns was back at the lodge twenty minutes later." She glanced down, "Officer Meirick was on duty starting at 8:00 am in the front hall of the Lodge until the theft was discovered at about 4:30 pm. After the theft was discovered, Officer Johanns was sent to Holy Trinity Church with several officers from the Sunningdale Police to search the grounds and buildings of the church at 5:45 pm and..."

There was silence as the constable quickly glanced at another document, and then she said, "Unfortunately, Officer Johanns was struck by a car at approximately 6:15 pm while he was crossing Church Road on foot, returning to Ednam Lodge."

"The night of the theft?" asked Madeline.

The constable nodded.

"He was hit by a car the night of the burglary?" confirmed Madeline, hoping she sounded sad instead of extremely interested, "that was too bad. I hope it wasn't serious."

"He was seriously injured," said the constable, "He was hit by a car as he was leaving the grounds of Holy Trinity. The car that struck him was driven by the vicar there." The constable stopped and said, "Here's an interesting side note," and she read aloud, "'The vicar was so upset he went into shock and was taken to the hospital.'"

The constable quickly scanned the rest of the report, "There were two witnesses in the car behind the vicar, who reported seeing Mr. Johanns leave the grounds of Holy Trinity through the Windsor Gate on foot and start down Church Road towards Ednam Lodge." The constable glanced at Madeline, "Well, the witnesses said Mr. Johanns was actually running." She started reading out loud, "'The vicar reported he didn't see Mr. Johanns running across Church Road until it was too late, and his car struck Mr. Johanns, who was thrown to the side of the road. A neighbor called for an ambulance, and Mr. Johanns was transported to the hospital, but he never regained consciousness, and he died of a stroke three months later in a nursing home."

The constable scrolled through another document in the file and said, "There is one more mention of the second bodyguard," and she read aloud from the document, 'Officer Dick Meirick was subsequently assigned in December of 1946 as a sergeant to the Thames District, where he served until his retirement from Scotland Yard in 1949.'" The constable looked up, "Anyway, that's all I have for you on the bodyguards."

Madeline did find Leonard Johann's actions on the day of the theft unusual.

"Now that I think about it," Madeline said to the constable, "I'm fairly certain that Leonard was the name of the bodyguard who knew my grandfather. I have one last question; my final one I promise. I am assuming the bodyguards assisted the Sunningdale police once the theft was discovered? My grandfather told me about that night a long time ago."

"Your grandfather was there that night?" The constable arched her eyebrows.

"No, he just heard about it afterwards, back at the air base."

The constable pulled a page out of the file and, reading from it, said, "The Scotland Yard bodyguards immediately searched the earl's home after the theft was discovered, looking for the case of stolen jewelry, and they also searched the buildings and grounds of the homes near the scene of the crime, including Holy Trinity." The constable looked up, "That's all I have in the file. I know that members of the Sunningdale Police Department interviewed each member of the earl's household staff on three separate occasions, and the grounds of the golf course were searched that night and again several times the next day. The jewelry was never located, and the police found no evidence incriminating any of the household staff, or the bodyguards. It was concluded that the crime was committed by 'unknown outsiders.'"

"It must have been a difficult time for everyone," said Madeline.

"I am sure it was," said the constable, "I know a couple of men identified as possible suspects by the Sunningdale were brought in and questioned several times over the next two months, but there was no evidence that anyone from Sunningdale, or Ascot, or even London was involved. The crime was never solved," added the constable helpfully.

"I am wondering," said Madeline, "could I have a copy of your police report from the night of the theft? I would like to have it for my family history file."

The constable went through the file again and said to Madeline, "The police report is marked 'Classified,' so I can't give you a physical copy."

"'Classified'? You can't tell me what's in it?"

The constable smiled, "I already read or pretty much-summarized everything that was in it regarding the bodyguards, so you have most of the information we have."

"I appreciate your time. You were very helpful. I suppose I have enough facts to continue my search. Thank you."

The constable smiled pleasantly, "No problem. I wish you luck in locating Mr. Johanns' war records. Your best bet would be to visit the National Archives in Kew."

The constable watched as Madeline wrote down the name, and then Madeline stood up. "Thank you again for your time."

Madeline shook hands with the constable, and she left for her waiting cab.

Ascot

Ten minutes later Madeline was back in Shay's hospital room, and she asked Shay to take notes, and she gave a full report of her conversation with the constable.

At the end, Madeline said, "Shay, I think your questions were all great! But I couldn't get an actual copy of the police report since it's still classified. I am a little curious why the police report from that night is still classified."

"Me too," said Shay, "still, Madeline, this is going well, isn't it? It's great!"

"Absolutely. Tomorrow, I'll go to the library in Ascot tomorrow and check out the news in Sunningdale around the time of the burglary," said Madeline.

Then Madeline hesitated. To her, Shay seemed on her way to recovery, and her questions showed her thinking was clear. Maybe Madeline should slow down their 'investigation' a bit since Shay had been able to track and follow the ins and outs of the investigation. After all, the purpose of their 'investigation' was to get Shay involved and challenged by something which was happening. Still, she didn't want Shay to get too wrapped up in a fake investigation that would have no conclusion.

Madeline decided to drop going to the library in Ascot the next day. It was pointless to run around the countryside digging up old, unnecessary information. Shay was getting better, and that was the goal.

"I am sad that Kathleen is not here, she would have loved to talk to us about this," said Shay. "I know Kathleen was very smart, because she told me she was," she said with a sad laugh. "I'm glad that you are following up on this and going to the library where Kathleen worked. She would have been pleased you are going there. Please give my sympathies to her colleagues."

Madeline looked at Shay and changed her mind about going to the library. She would go to the library because it would make Shay happy, but this was absolutely it. She was done with sleuthing.

* * *

The next day afternoon, Madeline walked into the Ascot library on High Street. Like any library in the U.S., it was quiet, with floor-to-ceiling bookshelves and kindly librarians wearing glasses.

"Excuse me, and I hope it's not too much of bother, but I would like to read up on the local Sunningdale news a couple of days before Oct. 16, 1946, and a couple of days after," she said to the librarian.

The librarian had brown hair, quiet brown eyes, and was dressed all in pale-brown, sweater and brown slacks as well as brown boots.

"Yes, that is possible, and I am glad to help you, but copies of newspapers before 1980 have not been digitized. I can get you all set up with our microfiche machine, and you can go through old issues of newspapers that way."

The librarian showed Madeline how to operate the clunky microfiche machine. Madeline dropped her purse beside the library table and set to work, slowly scrolling through the old news. Nothing much had been happening in Sunningdale right before the burglary, just church socials and school events. Madeline almost missed a small story about a tragic accident in Sunningdale on Oct. 13th three days before the burglary. A Sunningdale man planting tulip bulbs had been killed in his garden by an unexploded bomb from the war.

Even gardening could be dangerous in post-war England.

Madeline also found a lengthy article about the Duke and Duchess's upcoming visit to Sunningdale and then the front-page stories about the couple the day theft, but she read nothing real new on the crime itself. She spoke to the librarian on her way out and explained that her sister Shay had met Kathleen, and that Shay sent her sympathies to her co-workers. Madeline's visit had been a waste of time, but at least she could tell Shay she had been there and delivered her condolences.

* * *

Sunningdale

Madeline called Shay on her way back to the club, "Well, I didn't find out anything new in the library. Nothing much happened in Sunningdale, except, of course, for an ex-king emperor and his wife showing up for a visit and getting robbed, which is quite newsworthy. There was also a guy killed by an unexploded bomb working in his garden, but that was about it."

"We are on such a fascinating search," said Shay. "I am so glad you came up with this idea."

"It is fascinating, isn't it?" said Madeline.

* * *

Boston

Felix called her while Madeline walked through the door of her suite. She set two bags of groceries, milk, cream, soda, and pastries on the counter and yanked her phone out of her pocket.

"Hey Madeline, how is Shay, and when are you coming home?" he said.

"Coming home? I don't think it will be much longer. Shay is becoming more like her old self every day.

"How can you tell?"

"She is flirting with the doctors."

"That's good to hear," laughed Felix. "We can still go to New Hampshire once you're back. There will probably be a couple of leaves still on the trees. Well, maybe one or two leaves."

Madeline didn't want to explain that she might be tied up getting ready to turn Coda

Gems over to new owners. "Yes, well, we'll have to see," she said as she emptied the grocery bags.

Felix didn't say anything, but Madeline could tell he didn't like what she said, but she didn't care.

"There's a chance that I could come and…" Felix began, and then she heard voices in the background. It sounded like several people had walked into his office. "I need to check on some things," said Felix, "Goodbye. We'll talk," and he hung up.

She hoped Felix wasn't planning to fly to London. If he did bring it up, she would have to tell him, nicely, that it was just not a good time to come to the UK.

* * *

London

Hannah called Basil late that afternoon. "I'd like to stop by and talk to you at 5:00," she said and added, as if it were an afterthought, "If that will be convenient."

Basil didn't bother to check his calendar, but said, "Yes, of course, that will be fine. I will see you at 5:00, then."

Hannah arrived ten minutes early for her appointment. The door to Basil's office was open, and he stood when she walked in. He noticed she glanced down at her gold Rolex; Basil knew by now that Hannah was always early.

"Hello, Basil," she said and sat in the chair across from his desk.

"It's good to see you," he said. Hannah glanced around his office and folded her hands in her lap, and then unfolded them, which was unusual, since she usually sat stock-still, like a statue, once she sat down. Something was up, thought Basil.

Basil waited for Hannah to begin; it was her meeting, after all.

"Do you have an update for me on anyone else besides this Luella woman snooping around the Windsor burglary?" said Hannah.

"No, I haven't heard anything. The teaser for the burglary feature that ran in *The Times* was…unfortunate," said Basil.

There was a long silence before Hannah said, "Yes, it was. If it was meant to stir prurient interest, then it succeeded. It was yellow journalism at its worst."

"Supposedly, her article was only about a theory, nothing more," said Basil.

"Of course," said Hannah.

Basil added, "Well, evolution is also called a theory, but we all know it's real."

Hannah didn't respond. She just folded her hands again in her lap.

"In case you might have heard a rumor that I have written a book," said Hannah, "it's not a rumor; it's true. The book is about my father's career and mine, of course. There is a bit in it as well about my grandfather of course. I am positive it will be a bestseller. It will be published in the UK in four months, and they are already negotiating for a US release, which should be huge."

Basil looked at her, wondering if her book could be the reason Hannah was so worried about any fallout from any new interest in the Windsor burglary that her father, supposedly a brilliant director general, had failed to solve. If so, her intense concern made some sense now. Not a lot, but some. Hannah was anxious about something. He hadn't had much luck in finding any useful information that might help Hannah, much of the recordings were garbled, and he was worried that she was worried. He'd go through them again and see if he could make sense of her phone calls again with a new audio security app.

"Well," said Hannah after a quick look at her gold watch, "Call me if you hear about any new interest," and she stood up and left.

* * *

Ascot

Shay was released from the hospital the next day, and when the two sisters walked in the door of their suite, a dozen pink roses from Jonah had just been delivered. Shay sent him a thank you text and went to the closet and rummaged through her luggage.

"It seems like I haven't worn real clothes for at least two years," she said as she slid into a pair of her ragged blue jeans and her favorite sweater, a dark pink.

That night, Madeline, Chip, and Shay went out to dinner at the Spotted Cow in downtown Sunningdale to celebrate, and they ordered and drank four bottles of champagne until the manager gently suggested, half an hour after the restaurant had closed and the cleaners were vacuuming the floors, that it just might be time to go home.

They went home.

Chapter Thirteen

Sunningdale

At 8:00 that evening, Abby called Madeline while she was working at the small table in the dining nook, and Shay was asleep in the bedroom.

"I got a call from Aaron at Neptune Diamonds fifteen minutes ago," said Abby. "He told me he's made his decision and would send an offer to buy Coda Gems shortly. I received it a minute ago, and I am forwarding it to you now."

Madeline's heart sank. She had thought it might possibly happen in the distant, gauzy future. But here it was; it was happening now.

"He is offering us $875,000 excluding inventory, which is not a bad offer, but we do need to make a counteroffer. I am thinking $925,000 would be good. If you agree, I'll send it to Stan, since lawyers always have comments, and then you and I can talk about it. Aaron wants our decision in two weeks."

Madeline didn't say anything at first, and then said, "Do you think he'll agree to $925,000?

"I am guessing yes."

"Did he say when he wanted to close?"

"In ninety days. It's a good starting offer," said Abby. "It is better than I expected. Call me back after you've reviewed it."

"I will," said Madeline. "Two weeks for a decision? That's not a lot of time."

"It's enough time," said Abby. "Aaron told me he wants to have a grand opening by Valentine's Day."

"A grand opening of our store on Valentine's Day? That would be a stab in my heart, pun intended."

"Madeline, if I was there, in the UK, I'd walk over now and give you a hug. This is hardly a surprise, though. I know this is difficult; it's difficult for me, too, but we need to be objective."

"The truth," said Madeline, "is that at the present moment I am incapable of objectivity."

"Start practicing," said Abby, and Madeline could hear her walk into her office with her cell phone. She knew Abby was about to sit at her desk and sort through the day's mail.

"I was hoping we'd have our store for at least three or maybe five more months," said Madeline. Time, what Madeline needed was more time to save Coda Gems.

Abby ignored the comment.

"I'll take a look at the offer," said Madeline, "and send you a text in an hour," and they hung up.

* * *

Madeline stared out the bedroom window at the gray horses huddled in a corner of the paddock, sleeping probably. She mindlessly doodled on her calendar, thinking about the painful task of clearing out her desk at Coda Gems, and then packing up her seven or eight boxes of diamond and gold testing equipment in the back hall closet, plus her overpriced gemological microscope that she hadn't used in two years.

A minute later, Shay walked in, rubbing the sleep from her eyes.

"I could hear you talking from the bedroom," said Shay. "What did Abby have to say?"

"Nothing much, just the usual sales update," said Madeline, and Shay went back to the bedroom.

Madeline opened her briefcase and grabbed a blank sheet of paper and made a list of the pros and cons of Aaron's offer. She had a list of over twenty negatives under the 'Con' heading.

There was only one entry under the 'Pro' Column.

Money.

She turned the page over; it was the page from Kathleen's stack of old news reports, the one with the scrawled word 'Why?' in black ink that she'd found so curious. Madeline read the short text again on Kathleen's page, not an article, just a fragment, a couple of sentences from an old newspaper report,

When she'd first skimmed Kathleen's stack of copies several days before, including the snippet, she'd been in a rush. She didn't know Leonard's name then, nor the description of the award, so it meant nothing to her. But it did now.

* * *

April 17, 1947: Buckingham Palace

"The Royal Victorian Order has been awarded posthumously to Leonard Johanns of Scotland Yard for extraordinary personal service to the monarch, by his Royal Highness King George VI. Leonard's sister, Mary Adams, accepted the posthumous award on her brother's behalf in a ceremony in the Palace Gardens. She said, 'my beloved brother Leonard would have been honored by the acknowledgment of his devoted service to His Royal Highness. I will treasure his medal with great pride and...'

Unfortunately, the fragment abruptly ended. Nonetheless, Leonard had performed such an important service that he received a medal from the King of the UK and its Dominions and the Emperor of India, and Madeline had to wonder, "Why?" Just like the person who'd scrawled that word on the page.

However, the fragment confirmed her belief about the thief; it had been the bodyguard, Leonard Johanns. It had to have been him. According to

Sunningdale's chief constable, Leonard Johanns' service had been 'ordinary.' But it hadn't been, he had done something extraordinary for King George VI. The question was, what exactly had he done? She was pretty sure she knew.

She put the page back in her briefcase and sat for thirty minutes, thinking. Was it possible that Leonard had taken the jewelry from Ednam Lodge on orders from Scotland Yard and MI5, so they could be given back to the new King George VI and his wife at Buckingham Palace? After all, such a scandalous scenario had been rumored at the time, but the rumor now made actual sense. It would also answer one of Madeline's initial observations, that law enforcement had not seemed particularly anxious to solve the burglary. Of course, they wouldn't have worked hard to solve it, since none other than Scotland Yard and MI5 had set it up and pulled it off, with the probable collusion of the Sunningdale police. And now it seemed that Buckingham may have been involved as well.

Madeline wondered if Felix had a source at Buckingham Palace, then stopped wondering. Of course, he did. Not that it mattered; there was no way she was about to call him out of the blue to talk about Royal Family scuttlebutt. Still, she did wish she could talk to him just for a minute or two, or three, maybe even five minutes. She missed him, and she felt a sharp pang of loss, and tears welled up in her eyes.

She pulled out her cell phone to call Felix but changed her mind after she glanced at the clock.

Abby was waiting for her response to Neptune's offer, so Madeline made another cup of coffee and printed off Neptune Gems' offer. She looked for a non-compete clause in the nine pages of legal language, and there it was. She and Abby would not be allowed to open a jewelry store in the Metro Boston area for five years.

Madeline scanned the offer again, and while the furniture and cut-glass display cases were included in the sale, at least she could pack up and take her framed Boston Symphony prints, not that she had a use for anything that had an 'air of Old Money' anymore.

Madeline texted Abby that the counteroffer looked fine, and she hit send. She sat back in her chair, staring blankly out the window. Coda Gems was about to be sold, and Madeline was without a plan to save it. She had nothing, her brilliant idea to save Coda Gems with estate jewelry had turned out to be a waste of time, just a beautiful pipe dream.

Abby called back five minutes later, "I realize this is hard for you, Madeline. I do wish there was another way out, but Neptune Gems is our only hope. We should take the offer and just make the best of it, that's all."

"Yes, it is very difficult. I know it's difficult for you too, Abby. I suppose then that we do have to make the best of it then, don't we."

"We gave it a good run, though, didn't we, partner."

"We did indeed partner," and the two women talked for a sweet thirty minutes about their favorite customers over the years that, for Madeline's, included a crusty widow and a lonely executive assistant, and they said goodnight.

Madeline thought she had resigned herself to the sale of the store, but now that the sale was imminent with an actual hard and fast date, she wasn't ready. She didn't know what she could do, but she knew she had to do something, something big, something very big; very big and very fast.

She finally went to bed, and drifted off to sleep, but it was an uneasy sleep.

* * *

Sunningdale

Madeline got up at six am even though she had barely slept. She was restless, and after a check-in on Shay and a quick shower, she paced up and down in the bedroom, and then went outside and down the curved path toward the horse barn. The three gray horses stepped out of the barn in the misty dawn light, and walked up towards the fence, watching her, but as she got closer, they wheeled and galloped back toward the barn.

Madeline was anxious to go back home to Boston, but she would never forget the Sunningdale Golf Club and their incredible suite, the beautiful magnolia trees, the shimmering golf greens, and even the gray, skittish horses.

But flying home to Boston wouldn't be the same, knowing that Coda Gems would be gone soon.

She blindly stared at the barn door; and felt a deep sadness for the loss of Coda Gems. She knew Aaron would of course change the name of Coda Gems, and after that every trace of her and Abby's beloved jewelry store would be gone forever.

She knew she could not just idly sit by while her store slipped away.

Madeline stepped on a short magnolia branch lying on the ground, and she picked it up and snapped it in half, the sound loud and satisfying in the quiet morning. She dropped the pieces to the ground. She knew then, at that moment, there was only one way to save Coda Gems. She knew her idea more than bordered on the improbable and, on the face of it, even the absurd, but it was the only solution available, so she had to at least try. She would forever regret it if she didn't try.

After all, she did have bits and pieces of important information about the burglary, which, when taken together, was enough for her to at least do something, anything. Which was good, because doing nothing was simply not an option.

The only way she could come up with enough money to save Coda Gems in time was to hunt for and then find the Duchess's stolen jewelry. After all, she had gathered significant information about that night, apparently more than anyone else. There would be sure to be a reward of some kind if the jewels were ever found, and it would probably be a big reward, so in that sense, her plan was perfectly reasonable, shrewd even. She would have to deal with the dicey part that it could turn out that Scotland Yard, MI5, and certainly Buckingham Palace had all played a role, but she would jump off that bridge when she got to it.

* * *

Madeline's had written her two-page <u>Overview: Assumptions and Questions</u> about the theft as the basis of Madeline's cognitive therapy plan to help Shay recover from her brain concussion. By now the two-pager

142

had a different role. Madeline was positive now that Leonard, the Scotland Yard bodyguard, had taken the Duchess's jewelry from the bedroom at Ednam Lodge, likely instructed by someone at a very high level at Scotland Yard or MI5.

Leonard certainly had the opportunity to pull off the theft, and the fact that King George VI had posthumously given him the Royal Victorian Order for personal service was a dead giveaway. It was him. It also proved that Leonard wasn't a slick, ordinary jewelry thief; he hadn't taken the jewelry for his personal gain.

All Madeline had to do was find out where Leonard had hidden the jewelry before he was hit by the vicar's car and knocked unconscious on Church Road.

She would take a quick look at Kathleen's copies one more time and talk to Shay. After that she would head for Holy Trinity church, the last place Leonard had been, and go through the rooms of the church, looking for a 17"x 16" charcoal gray case of jewelry. Madeline did not think of her hunt as an unlikely one; it wasn't as if she was looking for a needle in a haystack, the titanium case would be hard to miss.

For the next forty minutes, she skimmed Kathleen's pages in case she'd overlooked something important, but she hadn't. Madeline had all the available information. She spent the next two hours at the desk, thinking about Leonard and what could have happened the day of the jewelry theft. She came up with three different scenarios and, after half an hour, picked the last one. It was complicated, but the only one that made sense, so she'd go with that.

Madeline put the stack of copies of the news reports away, it was time to talk to Shay, who had gone the club's library for 'a good book', which would be either yet another one on whales, or a corset-busting romance novel. She called Shay and asked her to come to their room for a 'conference.'

* * *

Shay gave Madeline a dazzling smile when she walked into the bedroom of their suite five minutes later. "What's up on this beautiful, gorgeous day? What do you want to do this afternoon?" said Shay, pulling at the sleeves of her dark pink sweater. She looked tired, but at least the bruises on her face were almost gone.

"It's a long story," Madeline, "but I have to leave for Holy Trinity in a couple of minutes and check out a few things."

"I like long stories," said Shay, "especially ones that involve you walking into a House of God."

"You mean because I might get struck by lightning or something?"

"Something's up, isn't it? I can tell you are up to something. Remember, I've known you your whole life. What's going on?"

"I've just been thinking about things."

Madeline knew she had to tell Shay about her suspicions regarding the theft, since she had talked Shay into working with her on her made-up 'amateur sleuth' plan. Madeline just hadn't realized that she would turn her made-up plan into an honest-to-God actual hunt for the stolen jewelry.

"You know, I believe the theft was a sophisticated, well-planned, but complicated crime gone awry. I am now positive that the bodyguard, Leonard, was the thief, especially since I just discovered that in 1947, less than a year after Leonard died, King George VI posthumously granted him a significant honor, the 'Royal Victorian Order, which is for personal service to the monarch.' But for what exactly?"

"Don't look at me," said Shay, pulling at the sleeves of her pink sweater, "I have no idea what he did."

"I think I do. While we were working together on our big investigation, I've learned a lot, and I've thought and thought about it, and I am certain Leonard's award was for stealing back the jewelry in 1946 that belonged not to the Duchess of Windsor, but to the Crown. The plan would been for the jewelry to eventually turned over to George VI. That part, though, never happened."

"Good God," said Shay, and her jaw dropped. "A Scotland Yard bodyguard was the thief?"

"I am positive Leonard did it on orders from his boss at Scotland Yard, with the collusion of MI5; Leonard picked the time and took the case jewelry out of Ednam Lodge. It's the only explanation that makes sense, but then something must have gone wrong right after, and the jewelry vanished."

"What went wrong?"

"Well, if the theft was as well planned as it appears to have been, Leonard should have handed off the case of jewelry to an accomplice as soon as he left Ednam Lodge. Then, this accomplice would have whisked the case of jewelry far away from the scene of the crime, and Leonard would have simply walked back into the lodge. But I don't think that happened."

"You really think Scotland Yard and MI5 were involved?" asked Shay, her eyes wide. "If this is true, it would be a huge..." and Shay paused, searching for a word, then said, "blockbuster of a story."

"Yes, it certainly would be. That day in Sunningdale, before the theft was discovered, Leonard left Ednam Lodge while he was on duty for an 'unexpected errand.' He went to Holy Trinity and was gone for twenty minutes," said Madeline, speaking quickly. "I've thought about it, and I think he had the case of jewelry with him when he left, but...and this is a big but...what if the accomplice never showed up? What if the accomplice was delayed? Leonard would have had to do something with the case of jewelry, since he could hardly take it back to Ednam Lodge. I am guessing he must have temporarily stashed it somewhere, anywhere, because he would have had to get back right away to his post at the lodge, and I know he was gone for a total of only twenty minutes, so he had to quickly hide it. Then, a couple of hours later, a maid at Ednam Lodge discovered the case of the Duchess' jewels had been stolen, and the police were called. Then, I know Leonard went back to Holy Trinity as part of an 'all hands on deck' law enforcement search party for the jewels, so he would have desperately needed to find a more secure place for the jewelry until the accomplice could return." Madeline paused to take a breath and continued, "But on his way back to Ednam Lodge, Leonard was hit by the vicar's car. I also know he didn't have the case of jewelry with him when he was hit by the vicar's car. So that's why," ended Madeline, "I need to go to Holy Trinity because the jewelry has to be in the church, or somewhere near there and...."

"Well, that is a bit confusing. So, when do we go to this church?"

"Shay, there is no 'we.' I'm going there, by myself, for a look around, that's all. You can't come because you are still recovering from a brain concussion, for God's sake. I have to go alone."

"But I should go with you," insisted Shay, "It will be dark soon, and you shouldn't be wandering around all by yourself."

"Don't be ridiculous. I'll be fine, and you absolutely cannot come with me to the church. I won't be gone very long. I have to leave in a couple of minutes," and Madeline stood up, "alone."

"I'm coming with you."

"Shay, stop being so stubborn. You can't! You just got out of the hospital, and you could trip and fall and end up with another concussion. Or worse."

"You can be such a drama queen," seethed Shay. "I am going with you."

"No, absolutely not! Don't be stupid, you can NOT come with me. I am serious, you can't come, it's just too risky," ended Madeline, raising her voice.

Shay stepped back and sighed, "Fine then, just let me know when you get back. You are an idiot, you know," and she stormed out the door.

* * *

Madeline sighed and walked down the long hallway, past the deli, and up to the front door looking for Shay, but didn't see here. Where did she go? She checked her watch, turned around, and noticed Jonah sitting at a bar stool at the end of the counter, in blue jeans and a black Harley Davidson sweatshirt, eating what looked like a kale salsa, the rosettes of the vegetables' a dark, vibrant green. Madeline had become an expert on kale because of Abby, who was very particular about her kale.

"Jonah," said Madeline, walking up to him, "Did you see my stupid single-minded sister walking past just now?"

Jonah shook his head no. "If I see her, I'll tell her you are looking for her," he said. "I am sorry I couldn't help you with your 'investigation.' The mystery of the stolen jewelry all but ruined my father's life."

Before she could ask him what he meant, his cell phone rang and he took the call, listening closely, and said "yes" four times in succession and disconnected. He turned to Madeline and said, "I have to go," and as he walked away down the hall to his suite, he said over his shoulder, "Don't set off on a pointless search for those stolen jewels and..." He stopped and added, "It could be dangerous."

Madeline watched him walk away. What was that supposed to mean?

Madeline went back to her suite, and in the little kitchen saw Jonah's copy of *The Times* she had dropped on the counter a couple of days before. Madeline picked it up and glanced at the front page. It was hard to miss Luella's s teaser under the bold "Upcoming Features" headline in twelve-point type. She read the short teaser, poured herself a cup of Death Wish, then read it again five more times.

So, someone else had shared her instinct there was something very 'off' about the burglary of the Duchess's jewels, as well as definitely 'off' about the investigation. The writer had sensed what Madeline had suspected, there had been a crime that several layers of law enforcement did not seem anxious to solve. And what was the 'powerful institution' that had compromised the investigation? The writer could only have meant Scotland Yard, or MI5 or Buckingham Palace. Or maybe all three? Madeline had to wonder where Luella had gotten her information.

Madeline was uneasy, and an old trope from Watergate flashed into her mind, "It's not the crime, it's the cover-up." In this case, could it be that perhaps the reason the Duchess of Windsor's burglary was never solved was that a much more serious crime underneath would have been revealed?

Madeline wanted to read Luella Kloberdanz's article and went online but could not find it. What she found instead was an announcement that Luella had died in an accidental fall from a speeding train the day her teaser had run in *The Times*.

A minute later, she knocked on Jonah's door.

"Fancy seeing you again so soon," he said when he opened the door, "Come in."

She stepped inside, "I hope I'm not interrupting, but I have an important question: what did your father mean when he said, "Let sleeping dogs lie?"

"You already asked me that, remember?" he said brusquely.

"I know, and you didn't answer." She handed him his copy of *The Times* with Luella's teaser. "I'm pretty sure you've read it since this is your newspaper that you left in Shay's hospital room the other day. The woman who wrote this teaser died in an accident the day this teaser appeared in the paper. It seems to me that her death was a little too convenient; her article never was published, was it? The rumor this Luella woman referred to was probably the one that Scotland Yard and MI5 masterminded the jewelry theft from the Duchess of Windsor in 1946 on behalf of Buckingham Palace no less. It could have happened that way. I'm bringing it up because it never did strike me as a good, old-fashioned jewelry heist."

There was a long silence, but Jonah didn't say anything, then Madeline added, "Well, I thought I'd ask." As she headed to the door, she turned and said, "I couldn't help but be curious."

"It's not always a good idea to be curious," said Jonah.

Madeline said goodbye and walked out the door.

Chapter Fourteen

Sunningdale

The constable at the Sunningdale Police Station called Basil at his office in London just after 4:00 pm that afternoon.

"This is Constable Sears with the Sunningdale Police," she said. "I've been meaning to call you since you asked to be notified if anyone showed up looking for information on that old Windsor theft. I thought you would like to know that an American woman came to the station, asking if we had any information on the Scotland Yard bodyguards with the Duke and Duchess of Windsor in 1946. She is in town, at least I assume she's still here, staying at the Sunningdale Golf Club."

"A woman showed up asking questions about the bodyguards from 1946?" repeated Basil. "Thank you for letting me know," he said, grabbing his notebook and a pen, "what is her name?"

"Her name is Madeline Lane and she is staying at the Sunningdale Golf Club," said the constable, and Basil wrote down the information in his notebook.

"What information did she want?"

"She wanted the names of the two bodyguards and anything else we had about them."

Basil heard several voices in the background, then the constable said," I have to go, there's been a break-in downtown," and she hung up.

* * *

London

Basil called Hannah immediately and told her of the conversation with the constable and about the American woman snooping around.

"The good news," said Basil, "is the woman, Madeline Lane, is staying at the Sunningdale Golf Club."

"This is an emergency situation," said Hannah in a harsh voice, "a very critical one that involves national security, and Basil, I need you to do something very important for me. I need you to drive down to the club in Sunningdale right now. Use your badge and get someone on the staff to ID this Madeline woman for you. Then, I want you to follow her and keep me posted on where she goes and who she sees. You need to go there right now, this minute. And hurry. Please."

Basil hesitated. He knew there was no way Hannah should be telling him to flash his badge, much less follow anyone, but he decided not to call his old mentor, Tisha. Yet. Something important was going o,n and the best way he could find out what it was would be to be in the middle of it. He also did have to wonder why people were now so interested in the Scotland Yard bodyguards from that old jewelry theft.

"No problem," said Basil, "I'll leave right away."

* * *

Basil called his office and told his assistant he was coming down with the flu and he was going home. Except he did not go home, he got in his car and drove to Sunningdale. However, he was held up by a car accident a mile in front of him for an hour, and while he waited in the line of stalled traffic, he had time to be nervous about following anyone around, especially an American, just because Hannah told him to. He called Tisha.

They spoke for nearly an hour, and he told Tisha about his concerns and admitted to her that he'd eavesdropped on Hannah's conversations lately, although he'd called it 'accidentally overheard,' and that he had tapped into several of Hannah's calls on her burner cell phones, which was hard to describe that as 'accidental' so he didn't.

"I was concerned," he explained to Tisha, "that something was going on, and I tried to identify the threat. There was lots of static on her calls, but I was able to pull out words here and there. I got the impression there is someone called The Patron who appears to be calling the shots in some sort of conspiracy, someone with a lot of money and a lot of contacts," he told Tisha.

"Thanks for the information," she said, "I am glad you mentioned this shadowy person, whose nickname is The Patron. I have recently become aware of that nickname, and that person is connected to suspicious activity by ex-MI5 employees. Do not mention this conversation to anyone," and she hesitated.

"Tisha, what is going on?" he prompted.

"New information has started coming in. That's all I can say for now. I'm trying to make sense of it."

"Do you mean 'all hell is breaking loose?'"

"Yes, that's exactly what I mean."

* * *

Sunningdale

In her suite at the club, Madeline got ready to leave for Holy Trinity. She changed into black slacks and a big black hoodie with a big kangaroo pocket in front, and a black beret. Next, she hunted through Shay's luggage for her sister's trusty Nikon and slung it around her neck, which was Madeline's idea of camouflage. Nothing screams tourist like a camera. At the last minute she glanced out the window and grabbed a raincoat.

Madeline decided to walk to Holy Trinity instead of showing up in one of

151

the club's cars because she wanted her arrival to go unnoticed. She didn't need a map; it was hard to miss the towering spire of the imposing church. Forget divine comfort; the two-hundred-year-old Gothic church looked grim and unforgiving in the pale afternoon sun.

* * *

As Madeline walked up to the church, she saw three cars pull into the parking lot. Doors slammed as women in sweatpants and T-shirts marched towards a side door of the church, a little casual, she thought, for a Church of England service. She caught up with a woman in the rear, in blue jeans and a sweatshirt, her bright red hair half covered by a bright orange scarf.

"Excuse me, is there a service in the church about to begin?"

The woman laughed, tugging at her orange scarf, and Madeline wondered if she had looked in the mirror before she left.

"At this time of day?" the woman said. "No. We are here to put a second coat of wax on the vestibule floor. The next service is tomorrow morning at 8:30."

The woman joined a group of other women waiting by the side door, and Madeline watched as one of them reached up to the lintel, took down what must have been a key, and unlocked the door. It should have occurred to Madeline that the church would be locked, but it didn't matter now. She knew how to get inside.

Madeline wanted to follow the women into the church, but she didn't exactly look like a volunteer parishioner. She looked like a tourist; she would have to come back later. She set off back to her room at the club. After five minutes, it started to sprinkle, which soon turned into a soaking rain, and she was glad for her raincoat. She sat at the desk outside the bedroom and scrolled through her cell phone, answering old texts. Madeline called the front desk and asked if they'd seen Shay, and was told that she was in the library.

* * *

Thirty long minutes later, Madeline left a note for Shay, picked up a sandwich at the club's deli, and walked back down Church Road to Holy Trinity. The parking lot was thankfully empty this time, and she took five 'touristy' photos of the front of the church in case anyone happened to be watching.

Madeline went around to the side door, and on her tiptoes ran her fingers lightly along the lintel above the door, but there was no key. She started over again, slowly this time, and halfway across felt a small, cold key. She slipped it in her palm, and in one motion turned the key in the lock and with a quick twist pulled on the wrought-iron handle.

The door swung open, and she stepped inside a dim, chilly vestibule of cold tile floors and soft gray walls. In front of her, three doorways loomed in semi-darkness. Madeline walked through the door on the right to a set of light switches on the wall. She clicked on two switches, and a soft light bathed the interior of the Anglican church. She stepped into the deep silence to rows of stately pews and glimmering stained glass windows and an imposing gray altar in the front, with several stark white marble statues off to the side, all very 'high church'.

She walked down the main aisle to the nave, not bothering to check under the pews, and then went through a side door to the sacristy. A wide table stood in the center, and the walls were lined with cupboards and drawers. It made no sense to rummage through those looking for a titanium case after all these years. She slipped down a set of wooden stairs to a large dining hall and a utility room with a huge furnace. There was no place a charcoal gray case of jewels could have stayed hidden for over eighty years. She hurried back up the stairs to the nave and turned to the front doorway. At the far end of the church, a mahogany choir loft gleamed above the wide entryway. Would Leonard have checked out the choir loft as a place to temporarily stash the jewels? Maybe, even though members of the church choir would have been in and out of the chair loft every week. She hurried down the aisle to an old and rickety spiral staircase in the foyer leading up to the choir loft.

Upstairs, there was nothing in the choir loft except for a large black organ, a narrow organ bench, and a stack of folding chairs. At the end of the loft, above the nave of the church, was an old, equally rickety railing.

She set the Nikon camera on the organ bench and ran her fingers across the brick wall, the mortar yellow with age, but found no suspicious chinks or cracks.

She went back down the staircase and then down a second small staircase to the basement and quickly surveyed the boiler room and an old-fashioned kitchen, which had walls of cupboards that she didn't bother with, and she ignored the dining room as well. These rooms were public rooms, with throngs of people going in and out of them on a weekly basis. She hurried down a hall with shovels, rakes, and gardening stakes hanging on the wall and opened the doors of three storage rooms filled with lawnmowers, hoes, and trash barrels. And then she was done.

Madeline hadn't really expected to find the duchess's jewelry in Holy Trinity church, but at least now she was reasonably sure the case of jewelry hadn't been hidden there. Where should she go next? The case of jewelry had to be somewhere close by.

* * *

Basil called Hannah, "I just arrived in Sunningdale. I went to the golf club and asked the man at the reception desk about Madeline Lane. He told me she had headed off on foot, with a camera around her neck, about half an hour ago. He said it looked like she was heading toward Holy Trinity. He showed me a copy of her US passport, so I know what she looks like."

"She left on foot?" demanded Hannah, "she might still be there. Get to the church right away and let me know when you find her," and she hung up.

Chapter Fifteen

Sunningdale

Madeline slipped out of the side door of Holy Trinity church into the slim October sunlight and stopped, thinking about Leonard, the bodyguard. He would have been frantic to find a more secure hiding place for the jewelry. Since Leonard had not found one inside the church, he must have been desperate. So where would he have gone? The two witnesses who saw Leonard Johanns get hit by the Vicar's car said they had seen him leave the grounds of Holy Trinity and head down Church Road, a narrow street that ran parallel to the cemetery.

Fifty feet away, the heavy, wrought-iron front gate of the cemetery stood half open, and Madeline hesitated. Would Leonard have gone to the cemetery that night before he left the grounds of Holy Trinity, looking for a secure place to hide the case of jewelry? Possibly. Maybe. She at least had to check it out.

Madeline walked through the cemetery gate, a cluster of imposing mausoleums on her immediate left, flanked by gray statues of granite grief. As she cautiously picked her way further into the cemetery, one word came to mind: creepy.

* * *

Basil was relieved when he spotted Madeline standing by Holy Trinity's cemetery gate, and he watched as she walked through it. He stepped out of his car, quietly shut the door, and nonchalantly walked through the cemetery gate fifty feet behind her.

* * *

In the cemetery, Madeline wandered down a wide avenue of tombstones and then another, winding her way through the gravestones, looking around. She walked into the cemetery for another fifteen minutes and glanced at her watch. She did not see any place where a desperate bodyguard might have hidden a charcoal gray case of jewelry that had gone undetected for eight decades. She concluded she was wasting her time, and besides, it was starting to get dark.

To Madeline's left was a pedestrian gate leading out of the cemetery to Church Road. She headed toward the gate to a stone bench that stood under a stand of weeping willows, with three old tombstones off to the side. She brushed the leaves off the bench and sat down for a minute. Tomorrow was another day, but she would not come back to the cemetery; there was nothing here. Tomorrow, she would find another place where Leonard might have gone after he left the church. She gazed out over the sweeping view of Sunningdale below. She had to wonder if that made these plots more expensive. Possibly. She checked her watch. Shay must wonder what she was doing, so she called her, but Shay didn't pick up; she was probably sleeping, or still in the library. Madeline left a cryptic message that she had been held up but would call her when she got back to the club.

Madeline glanced at the nearest tombstone. The date of death was October thirteenth' but the year was covered by a greenish mildew. Where had she just seen that date? Then she remember, the library in Ascot the day before. Madeline stood up and pulled a handkerchief out of her pocket. She rubbed the greenish mildew off the granite tombstone, still wet from all the rain, and the year 1946 appeared. So, this was the grave of the unlucky gardener in Sunningdale, the man who had died planting tulip bulbs.

The headlights of a passing car illuminated a sign, Windsor Gate, hanging just above the exit, and Madeline stopped cold, surprised.

According to the witnesses in the Sunningdale Police report, Leonard had been right here on the night of the theft and had run out this very gate to Church Road, but minutes later, he had been accidentally hit by the vicar's car. A charcoal gray case of glittering jewelry had not been mentioned in the police report, and it certainly would have if he had it with him. Which meant Leonard had obviously already hidden it in a great place. But where?

She thought about what Leonard might have seen as he was standing here by the gate. Were his eyes casting about, looking to see if anyone had followed him, or more likely, hoping to find a secure place to hide the jewelry case? She glanced around the cemetery; he would have seen rows and rows of tombstones, but on that particular day, on October 16, 1946, Leonard would have seen something else.

He would have seen the brand-new grave of the unlucky gardener twenty feet away, only a day or so old, likely not yet covered by a blanket of sod. The casket would have already been lowered into the grave by then, and on top of it would have been the mound of fresh dirt waiting to be covered by the sod.

Then Madeline had a morbid thought: desperate people do desperate things. Leonard would have been desperate that night of the theft to find a great temporary spot for the case of jewelry. Leonard would have needed a great temporary spot only until the intense police activity had stopped, and it could be handed off to the delayed accomplice. So where had Leonard hidden it? Unless...unless Leonard had concealed the case of jewelry in the freshly turned soil on top of the unlucky gardener's casket.

A new grave would be a brilliant, positively brilliant place to temporarily hide the case of jewelry safe from the scores of law enforcement that would have descended on Sunningdale searching every nook and cranny for the Duchess of Windsor's jewelry case. Yes, it would have been a brilliant place, since no one would ever think to look in a new grave. It would have been easy for Leonard to dig into the freshly turned soil, he wouldn't have needed a shovel, since a stick, or a rock, or even his shoe would have worked. If that is what had happened, Leonard would have, of course, planned to return later that night for the jewelry or very early the next morning.

Madeline bent down and ran her fingers across the gardener's grassy plot, the earth damp and soft from the heavy afternoon rain. She glanced around to see if anyone was watching, but she did not see anyone.

Yes, it all fit; if the Duchess's jewels were here, hidden in a grave in the cemetery, and Leonard struck unconscious minutes after and then dead three months later, that would explain why the jewels had vanished, why they had seemingly dropped off the face of the earth. Except they had not, the jewels were quite possibly right under Madeline's feet.

Madeline knew there was only one way to find out.

She looked around; the sun had just set, and it would be pitch dark soon, and she sighed. She had no choice, she had to stay, she had to stay in a gloomy cemetery and dig in a dead man's grave in the dark. Right now.

First though, to dig she needed a shovel, and Madeline smiled. It was a small smile. She knew just where to find one. On the outside wall of the third storage unit in the basement of Holy Trinity. She started walking back to the church. Madeline abruptly glanced back once, thinking she heard something behind her. She thought she saw a flash of pink, but Madeline decided it was just a trick of the dying sun, and she kept walking toward the church, faster now.

* * *

Basil was getting tired of following Madeline through a dark, shadowy cemetery as she wandered past rows of old tombstones. His cell phone vibrated in his pocket, and he pulled it out. It was just a text from Hannah: "What is going on?" He didn't reply.

Then, in the dim light, Madeline suddenly appeared practically right in front of Basil, and he had to quickly step back as she walked in front of him, heading now towards the church. Basil followed her out of the cemetery gate and up to the church and saw Madeline pull something out of her pocket and open a side door. So, she had a key. He stood in the shadows and hesitated, not wanting to follow her into the church, unsure of what to do next.

Then two minutes later he saw Madeline shove the side door open and walk back out. But she did not leave the grounds of Holy Trinity, instead she headed back into the dark cemetery carrying a shovel, and what looked like a three-foot-long gardening stake with a sharp pointed end.

Basil called Hannah, "Madeline left the cemetery, went into the church for a couple of minutes, and just walked out, carrying a spade and a stake or something. She is walking back into the cemetery."

"I am leaving now for Sunningdale!" said Hannah. "Do not let her out of your sight for one second! I will be there in twenty minutes or so, maybe less. Keep me updated."

Basil wheeled around and followed Madeline into the cemetery again. He pulled out his phone and called Tisha, but disconnected before she picked up. Soon, he'd call remember back soon, once he knew what Madeline was doing in a damn cemetery with a shovel and something with a pointed end.

Chapter Sixteen

Sunningdale

Madeline worked her way back to Windsor Gate and the three aging tombstones, partially hidden from the road by towering oak trees. After she dropped the shovel and garden stake, Basil abruptly stopped twenty feet behind her, watching her from the shadows.

Madeline stood at the foot of the gardener's grave, covered with short, brownish grass. She hesitated, then apologized to…and she glanced at the gray headstone to… Tom Kleckner.

She looked carefully around, she didn't see anyone, and she heard nothing but the sighing of the wind in the trees. She picked up the gardening stake, a genius, last-minute idea, and stared at the grave. Madeline knew the dimensions of a standard casket were 7' x 2', so she mentally marked out that area.

She had no time to dig up the entire layer of dirt on top of the unlucky gardener's casket. However, by easing the stake into the dirt, she could quickly find out if there was a charcoal gray metal case buried above the casket, or fairly quickly, she hoped.

Madeline eased the pointed end of the stake into the damp earth about three inches, and it came to a dead stop. She had to lean and push hard a couple of times before the stake slid deeper into the soil. She pulled it out and, with a heavy thrust, drove it deeper into the soil, at least ten inches, but did not hit anything. She moved to another spot twelve inches away and settled on the mechanics of her search with the metal stake: slide, push, heave, and ram it into the soil at least a foot down. Nothing.

Madeline tried two more spots, working her way up to the granite headstone. The work was hard, and even in the cool fall night, sweat dripped down her face.

She wanted to stop, but she couldn't stop, not now, not yet. Madeline was on the hunt, and she thought of Felix.

* * *

Basil's cell phone vibrated with a text from Hannah: "What is Madeline doing now? Where are you?"

Basil replied, "In the cemetery, at Windsor Gate. It looks like she's probing with a stake or something, shoving it in a grave. It looks like she's searching for something."

"What? What? Watch her! Do not leave. Stay in touch," said Hannah, her voice clipped and hard. "I am fifteen minutes away."

Basil sent Tisha a short text, "That woman, Madeline, is probing with a stake in a grave at Holy Trinity."

Tisha sent Basil a text reply, "What? Call me right away!" But Tisha's text was not delivered.

* * *

As she stood over the grave, Madeline had a quick, depressing thought: what if she was not shoving the stake deep enough? Possibly. If the titanium case was there, it might have been buried deeper, or it could even have just settled deeper into the dirt over time. She had no choice but to go back and start over at the bottom of the grave, this time jamming the stake two feet into the soil, stopping every couple of minutes to lift her head to look around.

The only sound in the cemetery was her heavy breathing. Twice however she thought she heard footsteps and froze, but it was nothing. Madeline wiped the drops of perspiration off her face with the sleeve of her hoodie.

Five minutes later, halfway up the left side of the grave, Madeline's gardening stake hit a hard object. She tried again four inches away and then tried four inches on the other side. Yes, there was something solid in the grave, something not tiny. It could just be a rock. Or not.

She turned and picked up the spade, and cut out a square of grass, cringing at every snick of the spade as it slid through the dirt, and she set the square of grass behind her. A throbbing pain began to radiate up her arms and down her back. After five minutes Madeline reached her bare hands into the grave, trying not to think about what she was doing. Then, she felt something, not a clump of hard dirt and not a rock. Something was there, at least a foot long, and it was smooth and hard.

* * *

Basil couldn't figure out what Madeline was up to, so he inched closer and tripped over a short, thick oak root snaking up out of the ground, and he fell to the damp ground, hitting his head on the gnarled root. Shaken, he slowly got to his knees, running his hand over a painful lump on his forehead. He massaged it, his head now throbbing, and his eyes out of focus. He was too dizzy to stand, and he stayed on his knees, swaying from side to side.

* * *

Madeline shone her flashlight into the hole she'd made in the grave and saw something shiny, something smooth and dark gray. She reluctantly reached into the hole again and felt a hard edge. Her pulse racing, she dug out more dirt with her fingers, and by getting down on her hands and knees, she was able to wedge both of her hands under the object. She twisted and rocked, and whatever was in the ground moved a couple of inches. She sat back, took a couple of deep breaths, and reached in again with both hands, pulling up as hard as she could.

At that moment, Madeline heard the roar of a speeding car barreling down Church Road only fifteen feet away, and two blazing headlights pierced the darkness, apparently heading right towards her. Madeline gave a mighty heave to loosen whatever was in the grave, and she felt the object abruptly give, and she fell backwards to the right of the grave. Madeline's breath had been knocked out of her, and she lay still, holding the object tightly against her chest.

* * *

Basil shakily stood up, and he stared after the lights of the car speeding down Church Road and looked around. He could not see Madeline anywhere. Where was she? Where had she gone?

* * *

As Madeline lay half on and half off the grave, she could still hear the sound of the car but didn't move. Her heart pounding, she continued to hold tight to whatever she had just yanked out of the grave, listening. Had the car turned around and was coming back? No, the sound of the engine was growing fainter. She continued to lay still, waiting, just in case.

With one hand, she shook the box, and she heard the clanking sound of metal against metal.

Madeline glanced around before she slowly got to her feet and brushed the dirt off a charcoal gray metal case. She sighed deeply before she slid it in the deep kangaroo pocket of her hoodie. She shoveled dirt back on the grave and tamped back the square of sod she'd cut out of the grave. Madeline tossed an armful of leaves and a couple of small branches to mask the disturbance on the grave. It looked relatively fine.

Madeline picked up the shovel and threw it over the cemetery fence into the shrubbery that ran along Church Road, and then tossed the gardening stake behind her into a row of bushes. Only then did she heave a sigh of relief.

* * *

Under the tree, Basil shook his head and rubbed his eyes, he still had difficulty focusing and his head continue to pound. Then he saw Madeline standing on the side of a grave, looking around. He ducked out of sight.

* * *

Madeline turned to walk out of Windsor Gate to Church Road when she had a horrible, devastating realization. Prominently sitting on the organ bench in the choir loft of the Holy Trinity Church was Shay's Nikon camera, her name and cellphone number taped on the outside of the camera case.

Madeline had no choice, she had to turn around and go back inside the church and grab the camera. She did not want the police or anyone quizzing Shay about anything. The police might even take her down to the station to find out why she had been prowling around inside a locked church. God knew what Shay might tell them.

Madeline suddenly thought she again heard a very slight sound of footsteps behind her, and she stopped, listening. Was someone following her? She heard nothing; it must have been the wind.

Madeline gritted her teeth as she brushed dirt from a grave off her hands and blue jeans as best as she could. She patted the comforting bulge of the charcoal gray case in the kangaroo pocket of her hoodie. She set off walking back through the cemetery, towards Holy Trinity; it was less noticeable than walking down Church Road.

* * *

Basil suddenly saw Madeline just ahead of him, walking through the cemetery, and relieved, he called Hannah. "I see her now; she's heading out of the cemetery; it looks like she's walking up to Holy Trinity."

"Is she carrying anything?"

"No."

"What is she wearing?"

"Jeans, a black hoodie, a beret, and short, blonde hair." Basil's voice was now a nervous staccato.

"Watch her," texted Hannah. "Watch her closely! Do not lose her! I am just a few minutes from the church."

Basil blinked furiously and rubbed his eyes again. He watched Madeline as she walked up to the side door of Holy Trinity and stepped inside the church.

He called Hannah, "She just went in the side door of the church. It's the door to the left of the main entrance."

Hannah replied, "You are doing a great job Basil, a really good job. I am driving into the car park now. Stay outside and keep watch. After I park, I am going into the church. Let me know right away if anyone else shows up."

* * *

As Basil neared the cemetery gate exit, he heard the crunch of tires in the parking lot, but he saw no lights. It must be Hannah.

He waited under a huge elm tree and watched as Hannah parked her car and saw her get out of it. After carefully looking around, he watched her try the side door of the church, and then step inside.

Basil pulled out his cell phone and called Tisha, but she did not pick up. He left her a short message that he was outside Holy Trinity Church in Sunningdale, and Hannah had just arrived. He walked around to the front door. Maybe Hannah was expecting him to wait in the front?

Chapter Seventeen

Sunningdale

Madeline was careful when she opened the side door of the church and did not turn on the lights. She walked into the vestibule in the dark, felt her way over to the choir loft stairs, and quietly made her way up the rickety staircase.

Despite her caution, the stair steps creaked, and she stopped, listening. Then Madeline thought she heard a door softly close on the first floor below. Was someone there? No, that was just her imagination again. Only after she waited on the stairs for two minutes did she climb up the steps.

Once on the landing, she stared into the darkness of the loft. She thought she had picked out the black shadow of the organ, and for five minutes, she edged her way toward it, but where was the organ bench? Shouldn't it be right...? And she stumbled against it, and the bench tipped over on the floor with a crash. Madeline went down hard on the loft floor but got back to her feet immediately, the pain in her left knee deep and throbbing. In the hard silence that followed, Madeline held her breath.

She decided this was ridiculous; she had to see, and she remembered there was a wall switch beside the organ. She crawled over to it, inching her way up the wall, and clicked it on.

The harsh glow of overhead fluorescent lights flooded the loft. Shay's camera lay in front of her on the floor and she grabbed it. She patted the kangaroo pocket of her hoodie, and her heart stopped, the kangaroo pocket was empty! The case of jewelry must have fallen out when she fell, but where was it? Then Madeline turned and saw the titanium case on the floor a foot behind her.

Madeline had to blink several times in the glare of the lights and then heard a sound of muffled footsteps on the choir loft stairs. She turned her head and looked behind her.

Madeline recognized the grim, unsmiling woman standing on the landing, a snub-nose revolver in her hand, pointing at Madeline. It was Hannah Davis, the woman from MI5, the one with the gold Rolex in that British business magazine. What on earth was she doing here?

"I know where you've been," said Hannah. "I know what you found in the grave. I've seen photos of the Duchess' jewelry case. Hand it to me, and don't make any sudden moves." She waved the gun. "Hurry up, or I'll shoot. Nobody's around to hear it."

Madeline froze and then was aware of a soft, very slight sound on her left, so slight she almost didn't hear it, less than ten feet away.

Out of the corner of her eye, in the dim shadow of the pipe organ, Madeline caught a glimpse of pink and a face framed by flowing brown hair. She could only stare. It was Shay, it was her, it was definitely Shay. As Madeline watched, Shay started to walk out of the shadows toward her.

Madeline had only a panicked second to react.

She turned and grabbed the gray titanium case behind her, brandishing it in the air as she shouted to Hannah, "You want this? If this is what you want, come and get it."

Madeline heaved the titanium case into an opposite corner of the loft and clicked off the lights. In the dark, the gray metal case hit the brick wall with a loud clang. Madeline could hear Hannah start towards the case in the dark, and then she heard Hannah lose her balance and lurch forward as she tried to regain it. The momentum sent Hannah crashing toward the choir loft railing four feet away. She could hear Hannah break through the fragile railing and fall with a sickening thud to the marble floor twenty feet below.

Madeline clicked on the lights and stared down at Hannah, motionless on the marble floor below the loft, her head twisted at an unnatural angle to the left.

"I'm glad I found you," said Shay, her face rimmed with exhaustion as she walked up to Madeline and said, "Who were you just shouting at? What was all that noise?" She looked around, dazed, "I'm glad the lights came back on."

Madeline said, "I can't believe you followed me."

"I had to. Why were you in a cemetery? What was all that noise?"

Madeline stepped in front of her so Shay couldn't look down and see Hannah lying on the floor below; Madeline was not sure what Shay had seen or overheard.

"I had to check out the date on a tombstone is all. You must go back to the club now, I can tell you need some sleep. Go back to the club. I'll be there in a few minutes. That noise was just my cellphone, a butt-dial or something."

Shay looked around and Madeline walked with her to the choir stairway and said, "Everything is fine Shay," and kissed her on the cheek, "but I need you to go back to our room at the club. Now."

Shay glanced around the choir loft, nodded, and tiredly slipped down the loft steps. Madeline watched as Shay went out the side door below, and then Madeline rushed to the staircase.

* * *

As Madeline started down the loft staircase to Hannah, still motionless on the floor below, a red-haired man in a black uniform ran in the side door and up to Hannah. He punched a number into his cell phone and looked up at Madeline when she was halfway down the loft staircase. She stopped.

She heard the man shout into his phone, "Send an ambulance to Holy Trinity immediately. The front door will be unlocked. No sirens. Repeat, no sirens. I am with Hannah Davis, and she just fell from the choir loft here and is seriously injured. Hurry."

He looked up and said to Madeline, "Ms. Lane, I am Officer Basil Talbot from MI5. Come down here now, please," as she walked up to him, he flashed an ID card and shoved it back in his pocket. She shivered as she watched him kneel beside a motionless Hannah, checking for a pulse.

Madeline saw Basil lean over Hannah's body and pocket the snub-nosed handgun lying next to her right hand.

"A colleague will be here shortly to speak to you," he said.

"How is she?" asked Madeline, nodding to Hannah, still motionless.

"She is alive, that's all I can say. The EMTs will be here soon and take her to hospital."

"How do you know my name?"

"The police in Sunningdale told me. I saw you in the cemetery tonight, with a shovel, standing beside a grave. What were you looking for?"

"I was walking in the cemetery, and I was curious about the date of the man's death," said Madeline, as if that explained everything. She clasped her arms around her sides to keep her hands from shaking.

Basil turned away, checked Hannah's pulse again, and punched in another number on his cell phone.

* * *

Madeline turned and rushed up the stairs to the choir loft, scooped up the charcoal gray jewelry case and shoved it back in the kangaroo pocket of her hoodie. This time she closed the snap. She also grabbed Shay's camera, slung it around her neck, and went back downstairs. Basil was still kneeling beside Hannah, not taking his eyes off the unconscious woman.

"I have to leave now," said Madeline when she reached the landing, "I have a family emergency, my sister…"

Without looking at her he said, "This is now an MI5 matter, and you can't leave," and Basil went back to his call.

* * *

Long minutes slowly ticked by, and Madeline thought about just walking out the side door since there was no one to stop her. Then, three officers in black uniforms walked in, and she heard another car pulling into the parking lot.

She wished again that she could talk to Felix for a minute or two. Since that was not possible, she would just have to ignore it. That didn't work, and her longing turned into a dull ache, which was worse.

Five minutes later the front door of the church banged opened. Madeline watched as three EMTs rushed up to Hannah with a stretcher and carefully moved her onto it, then rolled it outside to a blinking ambulance.

* * *

Three minutes later, an attractive Black woman in her early thirties, in dark slacks and a white blouse, rushed into the church, spoke to Basil, and then walked up to Madeline. The woman showed her an MI5 ID card and stared at Madeline's jeans. Madeline glanced down and brushed off a big clump of muddy dirt.

"My name is Tisha Lloyd," she began. "I am with MI5, an intelligence agency here in the UK. The woman who fell is Hannah Davis, the former Director General of our agency. We are taking her to a government hospital in London." She gave Madeline an appraising look with her pale brown eyes, "Why are you here in Holy Trinity?"

"I came to the church to pick up my sister's camera," said Madeline and lifting up Shay's Nikon around her neck. "I can't believe that woman fell through the railing. I don't know why she..."

Tisha interrupted, "My colleague Basil Talbot, from MI5, was standing just inside the front door, and he saw her stumble and fall from the choir loft. Did you witness it as well?"

"No, I was in the choir loft and then the lights went out, but I did hear her lose her balance in the dark and then I...I heard her break through the railing and fall to the floor below. I know who she is, but I don't know why she is here."

"I am part of an ongoing MI5 investigation," said Tisha. "I can't comment on it further except to say it involves Hannah Davis. Can you please come with me outside, and we can talk in one of our cars?"

Tisha turned and went down the stairs and Madeline followed her outside to one of the four black and white cars in the parking lot. Tisha got in the back seat and motioned to Madeline to slide in beside her.

"How is the woman doing?" asked Madeline.

"Her injuries appear to be serious, but I'll ask the questions if you don't mind," said Tisha, "and then if I can, I'll answer yours. My colleague Basil told me that you were in the cemetery tonight looking for something in a grave. Can you please elaborate?"

Madeline nodded. She knew the jig was up, sort of. So, she would tell the truth, sort of. "I am fascinated by the story of the Duchess of Windsor's stolen jewels, and when I was walking through the cemetery, I saw a grave with a 1946 October date of death, and I wondered if maybe, by some weird stroke of fate, the jewels were hidden in the grave, so I poked around a bit and realized it was a stupid idea. After a couple of minutes, I left and walked back to the church to pick up my sister's camera."

"You are curious about the Duchess' stolen jewelry?" said Tisha.

"Yes, I'm in the jewelry business."

Tisha sat back, eyeing Madeline carefully, "Why are you in the UK?"

"My sister was in an accident with a tow truck in Ascot and was seriously injured, and I flew to the UK to be with her. A local woman, Kathleen Large of Ascot, was killed in the accident."

Tisha's eyes shot up to Madeline's, "Your sister was in the vehicle with Mrs. Large?"

"Yes. My sister ended up with a brain concussion and was severely bruised, but she is out of the hospital. I will take her back to the U.S. in four or five days."

"I can tell you that Hannah Davis is under investigation," said Tisha, "for several very serious felonies, one of them related to the tow truck crash that killed Mrs. Large."

"You are saying that it wasn't an accident?" said Madeline.

"No, I said that it is under investigation."

Madeline looked toward the door, "I need to leave now because my sister is waiting for me at the golf club. She has not completely recovered from her concussion, and she is there alone. I need to get back."

"I'd like to see your identification."

"I don't have anything with me." Madeline's passport was in her jeans pocket, but she was not about to turn that over to this woman. Madeline suspected Tisha was a hard-ass cop who might take her time to give back her passport.

"Fine," sighed Tisha, "an officer will drive you to the club. I will come and talk to you more tomorrow morning. Don't leave town."

Madeline nodded, and after Tisha slid out of the car, the officer drove Madeline to the Sunningdale Golf Club. On the short ride, Madeline tapped the bulge of the charcoal gray case in her hoodie to make sure it was still there, but she was neither excited nor exhilarated. What she felt instead was a weary sadness and a sense of responsibility for the Pandora's Box of jewelry she had just pulled out of a grave.

She was one who decided to hunt for them, and she was the one who dug them up out of a muddy grave, so she was the one who would have to deal with the repercussions of her actions.

Funny how karma works.

* * *

Five minutes later, when Madeline walked into their suite at the Sunningdale Golf Club. Shay was sound asleep in her bed by the wall, and Madeline checked on her. Shay was not that many days out from a brain concussion, but her breathing sounded normal. Madeline set the charcoal gray case of jewelry in a dresser drawer. She went into the suite's small laundry room and threw her muddy jeans and hoodie into the washer. After she took a shower, she put on an oversized black t-shirt and crawled into bed, but she could not fall asleep. Madeline finally got out of bed and sat at the desk; Shay's biographies of the Duchess of Windsor were stacked on the edge. Madeline opened the top bio and, after skipping a couple of chapters, read that the Pasteur Institute, headquartered in France, had been the unexpected beneficiary of the Duchess' estate. Madeline was surprised by its history; the Pasteur Institute had been the first to develop lab-created vaccines for infectious diseases and had won ten Nobel prizes over the years. Well, that was impressive, very impressive, she thought as she set the biography back on the stack.

Madeline opened her laptop and googled Jonah Musgrave. According to the web, Jonah not only owned the Sunningdale Golf Club, but also four other private golf clubs in the UK, as well as five luxury hotel chains in France. She also read up on the two charities Jonathan chaired, one in the London and the second, *Doctors Without Borders*, headquartered in Paris.

Madeline sighed and clicked off her laptop; she now knew what she had to do.

Before she got into bed again Madeline emptied the Duchess' jewelry case on her bed. She put on every piece of the duchess' jewelry in the charcoal gray case; stacking all the rings on her fingers, covering her arms from elbow to wrist with gleaming golden bracelets, and she draped all nine necklaces around her neck. She ended by clipping the four-diamond and ruby brooches of the Duchess on her black beret.

Madeline stared in the mirror, and she laughed aloud. After all, there is nothing to soothe the soul like excess. After Madeline took off the jewelry and set the case of jewelry back in the dresser drawer, she got into bed and fell asleep immediately.

* * *

After Madeline woke up at 7:00, she put on her black hoodie and blue jeans, and her olive-green cowboy boots, her second favorite pair, and had a cup of Death Wish. She decided she needed another cup and after she was finished, she picked up the Duchess' case of jewelry and knocked on Jonah's door down the hall.

Since she didn't have his phone number, the only thing she could do was just show up.

"Good morning, Jonah, and sorry, I know it's early, but it's important," she said when he opened his door in baggy blue jeans and a gray sweatshirt.

"You do have a habit of just turning up. Come in."

He led Madeline through a large, sunny living room of Frank Lloyd Wright furniture and Art Deco stained glass windows and then into his office, a large room with floor-to-ceiling bookcases, a leather-topped desk, an Eames chair, and nothing else.

Madeline reached into her hoodie, and set the gray case of jewelry on his desk, "I did look for the Duchess' case of jewelry last night, and it's a long story, but I found it."

"Where?" asked Jonah, nodding to the charcoal gray metal case.

"In a grave in Holy Trinity's cemetery."

Jonah's gray eyes searched hers, his eyes expressionless; the man was unflappable. He said, a statement rather than a question, "You found the stolen jewelry in a grave in Holy Trinity's cemetery."

Madeline nodded.

"How do you know the jewelry is inside?" he said.

"Trust me, the jewelry is inside."

"This is ridiculous."

"It is, isn't it?" countered Madeline.

"How did you know where to look?"

"You warned me not to look for the jewelry," said Madeline, "you said it could be dangerous. That was an odd thing to say, wasn't it? Turns out it was very dangerous."

For the next ten minutes, Madeline told him about Shay's concussion and how Madeline ended up piecing together information on the robbery of the Duchess' jewels.

"I got involved in a fake search for the thief because I thought it could be a way to help my sister recover from her brain concussion because she's obsessed with rubies," said Madeline, "and it did help her. However, I got involved in the actual hunt for the stolen jewelry to save my store in Boston, because I needed $250,000 to save my store, and I thought a reward would be possible if I found the stolen jewelry. Once I had gathered enough information, I guessed where the jewelry had been hidden."

Madeline waited for his reaction to her explanation.

"Interesting," was his only comment, but then followed it up with, "assuming what you say is true."

Jonah picked up the titanium case and studied it. Madeline could tell he assumed it was locked. She wasn't about to mention that it wasn't, and she had already opened it. Why should she make anything easy for him? He went into another room and was back in a minute with a screwdriver, a hammer, a chisel, and a pair of pliers. Madeline stood by watching. But before working on the case with his tools, he tried the catch, and unexpectedly, the lid slid open.

Inside the titanium case lay a jumble of gleaming gold bracelets, necklaces, and rings studded with sparkling rubies, diamonds, emeralds, and sapphire gems. Jonah's eyes widened as he stared at the glittering treasure, then he looked at Madeline.

"I want to know," said Madeline, "why you said it was dangerous?"

Jonah watched her carefully, avoiding her question, but said, "Madeline, why are you showing me this?"

She didn't pick up the jewelry pieces and examine them, and neither did Jonah. Then Madeline reached across and closed the titanium lid.

"Why are you showing me this?" he repeated.

"It's complicated. First, I took it upon myself to find the jewels, and I did. Which means I now have a responsibility to see that the right thing is done. I want the jewelry to go to the Duchess' legal beneficiary, so I am asking you to help me."

"Me?"

"Yes, you. I don't know what else to do, and I know you are a resourceful man. The Duchess left this jewelry in her will to the Pasteur Institute, and I need to make sure this jewelry ends up there. Otherwise, greedy lawyers will be the ones to benefit.

"My point is, Jonah, I need to be out of the picture completely, totally, because I would be just a distraction, a very big distraction in this strange story. I'd be painted as a greedy 'American Adventuress' angling for a reward, which does have a bit of truth to it, but that's not important now. You know the British media coverage of me would be intense and hateful, and my life would be miserable. You realize that an American woman's story of digging up the most famous stolen jewelry in the world from a grave in Sunningdale, with her hand out for a reward, would create a huge media frenzy, the kind with big and nasty headlines. To be honest, I didn't really think the whole thing through at the time, and I now want out of the whole drama. I want to leave the jewelry with you because you can make what should happen...happen."

"What, in your opinion, should happen?"

"First, I think you should come up with a believable story, like you accidentally 'discovered'" the case of jewelry while you were upgrading one of the fairways on your golf course. It is a plausible story that the unknown thief hid them on your golf course right after the theft and for some reason never returned.

"No one knows me in the UK," continued Madeline, "but you are a well-known and well-respected business leader in the UK and in France, too. You've also done a lot of work with non-profits," and she smiled, "I read about you."

"Madeline, you are ready to just walk away?"

"Yes. I do not want my name and how I found them to be published, ever. I will, however, want your assurance that you will do your best to see that the jewels stay with the Pasteur Institute. That way I will have met my responsibility. That is all I want, no guarantees, no promises, just your best efforts."

Jonah sat quietly, studying Madeline. "I will have to think about what you told me. How do you know I won't sell them on the Black Market?"

"You could, but I don't believe you will."

"Who knows that you have the case of the Duchess's jewels?"

"No one knows for sure. Three people with MI5 know I was digging in a grave in Holy Trinity Cemetery, but none of them know for sure that I pulled the case of jewelry out of a dead man's grave. Well, Hannah Davis knows I did find them, because she recognized the Duchess of Windsor's jewelry case. I don't think that matters now because I'm not sure what physical or mental shape Hannah will be in when or if she ever regains consciousness." Madeline then described the confrontation with Hannah in the choir loft.

Jonah sat quietly, lost in thought, staring at Madeline.

"I do have one important question for you," she said to Jonah. "You mentioned a couple of times that your father said to 'letting sleeping dogs lie.' What did he mean by that?"

"I already told you he never told me what he meant," sighed Jonah.

"I know, but what did you think he meant?"

Jonah shifted uneasily in his chair, "From a couple of things my father said the year before he died, I was sure he believed that MI5 never wanted any real investigation of the 1946 burglary, and he suspected they were continuing to actively quash any in-depth inquiries. Once my father was certain that MI5 was involved and had likely masterminded the theft, I am positive that's when he completely backed away from looking for her jewelry. He even flat-out told me a couple of times over the years that dangerous people, very dangerous people, work at MI5, so I believe he was afraid. Intelligence agencies can be vicious."

"That would be a good reason why no one was anxious to solve it," said Madeline.

Jonah nodded again.

Madeline stood up, giving the Duchess' case of jewelry one last look, and turned to him. "I am leaving the jewelry with you now. I'm sure you have a very good safe here at the club."

"You will leave the jewelry with me and just walk out the door?"

"Yes, I am beyond exhausted. It has been a horrible, exhausting day, and my sister could have been murdered, so yes, I want to leave."

"You are an intrepid woman," he said, staring at her. "Yes, a very intrepid woman."

"If that's what you want to call it," she said.

Jonah stood up and walked Madeline down the hall to the door of her room. "You are doing a very good thing. I can promise I will make sure the duchess' jewelry ends up with the Pasteur Institute. I have resources." he said and flashed a quick smile.

"I believe you, and I trust you."

He kissed her on the cheek and waited until she had let herself into her room, and then he turned and went back to his suite.

Chapter Eighteen

Sunningdale

When Madeline woke up the next morning at 7:00, Shay was sound asleep in the next bed, so she went to their small dining room and called Felix, even though it was only 2:00 a.m. in Boston. Madeline needed to hear the sound of his voice, and she didn't want to wait until the sun came up in Massachusetts.

Felix answered on the second ring, his voice heavy with sleep, "Madeline, you are either in jail, or you just had a dream about me."

"Well, it wasn't a dream really," she said, "it was better, it was more of an epiphany. I'll be back in Boston in about five days, and I want to see you."

"Really?" he said, "About what?"

"Meet me at Logan Airport," she said. "I'll be naked under my clothes."

There was a pause, and he said, "You do know how to get my attention, even in the middle of the night."

Madeline heard Shay get out of bed and head to the bathroom, and she said to Felix, "I called you because I wanted to hear your voice and to let you know I'll be back home soon. Maybe we can go to New Hampshire one weekend soon after I get home? I really have missed you."

"All I can say is that must have been some epiphany."

"It was. Let's talk in the next couple of days. I have to go, but goodbye for now."

"I am glad you called, and I will be so very happy to see you. Goodbye, my love," said Felix, and they both hung up.

* * *

Since Abby was an early riser, Madeline called her at 6:30 am Boston time.

Madeline began by saying, "Well, I had an unusual afternoon and evening yesterday."

"What happened?"

"You remember I told you that I was getting Shay interested in the details of the burglary? What happened though was that I ended up putting two and two together," she continued, "and so I went looking for the stolen jewels, in a cemetery of all places, and believe it or not, I..."

Abby interrupted, "You went looking for the stolen jewelry? You told me the theft had been planned by criminal minds. You said that, remember?"

Madeline had no intention of telling Abby that the criminal minds that had planned it had been with MI5 and Scotland Yard.

"I said that? I was wrong. It was probably just the work of amateur burglars." Madeline cut corners in her rendition of that night, making it sound like she simply had a guess where the jewelry might have been hidden. She also left out that Hannah had demanded the jewels at the point of a gun. Abby didn't need to know that part.

Madeline ended with, "So anyway, believe it or not, I did find the jewelry case stuffed in the dirt above the casket, and I turned it over to Jonah Musgrave, who is a big deal in the non-profit world in France. He will personally take the jewelry to the Pasteur Institute since they are the Duchess' legitimate beneficiary. Also, yes, I did open the case, and the Duchess' jewelry is amazing,"

"It's an incredible story," said Abby, "I can hardly believe it. This could make you famous."

"Or infamous, since the British press will tear me to pieces if they ever get wind of my involvement, which is the last thing you or I would want."

"You are not in trouble with the British authorities or anything for digging in a grave?"

"What? No, they'll never know I was ever there. The story released to the press will be that Jonah found the case of jewelry on his property. I am totally out of the picture, and that's the way it will stay. It's just better for everyone that way."

"I can't believe you dug up a grave," said Abby.

"I didn't dig 'up a grave'" said Madeline, "I dug 'in a grave'. There's a difference."

"It's still a pretty unbelievable story," said Abby.

"It is, isn't it?" said Madeline.

Abby asked Madeline questions about how she knew where to look, and Madeline said, "The constable was very helpful, and I asked a lot of questions.

"Like what?" asked Abby.

"I have to go," Madeline lied because she didn't want to talk about it again, EVER, especially to Abby. "The MI5 officer is coming to talk to me," and the two hung up. Two hours later, Tisha called to postpone their meeting "due to evolving circumstances in the investigation. Can I call you on Thursday at 4:00 pm? If that is convenient?"

Madeline said, "Yes, of course," as if she was looking forward to it.

* * *

Over the next several days, Madeline went with Shay to Heatherwood Hospital to Dr. Marley for her daily eye and vision tests, and all was well. After the sisters got back to the club on Thursday, Tisha spent two hours with Madeline.

"Hannah Davis is not expected to ever regain consciousness and will remain in a long-term care facility for the rest of her life," began Tisha. "You remember I mentioned I have been coordinating with a team at MI5 monitoring former employees' activities. The team went back, way back for years, evaluating old MI5 reports, scouring old information, and they detected disturbing patterns at the Director General level, starting with Gregory Davis, Hannah's father.

"Gregory had a mysterious nickname back then used by most of his former

MI5 employees. They called him 'The Patron'. Gregory masterminded several, let's say, highly illegal operations to solve domestic security issues in the UK and he used blackmail and intimidation, as well as bribery to coerce former agency employees to help him. From time to time he even brought in Scotland Yard employees.

"Whether the correct people were tried, convicted, and sentenced in those security cases is now under scrutiny, but the upshot was that Gregory's reputation was magnified and inflated with every conviction. Then, it became clear to the team that his daughter, Hannah, used the same tactics of blackmail and intimidation, although it seems as if she resorted to murder in several instances. Oddly enough, she also used the same nickname, 'The Patron,' as she went about successfully 'solving' difficult MI5 cases.

"I am not sure how much of this will ever be public knowledge," said Tisha, "we are an undercover agency, after all. I can't comment any further on this matter, now or ever, but the agency deeply regrets any miscarriage of justice that may have occurred. Like I said, the investigation is ongoing and won't be completed for some time, and that is all I can say." Tisha suddenly smiled, "I do want you to be aware that I will not be investigating your actions in the cemetery because I do not believe what you were doing or what you found there is germane to my investigation."

Madeline stared at her, and Tisha nodded and looked away. That's when Madeline knew that Tisha didn't want to know any specifics of what had happened in the cemetery. Then Tisha added, "I am happy that your sister is recovering from her accident."

Tisha stood up, and Madeline walked outside with her to the waiting MI5 car. The two women shook hands, and Tisha slid into the back seat. The two women nodded their heads to each other as the car pulled away.

Madeline never heard from Tisha Lloyd again, except for a personal note, wishing her well, and she also wrote that she had promoted Basil Musgrave to her team as a VP Special Assistant.

* * *

Boston

Jonah was in touch with Madeline three times after she left the Duchess' jewels with him; the first time to send her a news clipping from *The Times of London* with the astounding news that the Duchess of Windsor's stolen jewels had been discovered buried in a fairway of the Sunningdale Golf Club by Jonah Musgrave, the club's owner. The second time, he sent her a copy of the Pasteur Institute's monthly newsletter, announcing that the Institute had received the Duchess of Windsor's lost jewels from British businessman Jonah Musgrave, which had been buried on his property since 1946. The Institute was "grateful and thrilled" to receive the jewels and promptly hired a team of probate attorneys to ensure that according to the terms of the Duchess of Windsor's will, the jewels were, in fact, the rightful property of the Institute. They will likely auction off the pieces to high-profile buyers to raise the maximum amount of money for the Institute.

The third time Jonah was in touch, he flew to Boston to take Madeline to lunch at the restaurant Mistral, and once they were seated, he handed her a certified check for $500,000.

She glanced at it, her eyes wide in shock, and she set it on the table.

"Why are you giving me this?" she said, looking at him.

"You deserve a significant reward," he said, nodding to the check, "because you are an 'intrepid' woman, and you deserve it. What you did will make a difference in thousands of people's lives. Besides," he said with a slight smile, "I am a very wealthy man, and I personally want you to receive a significant thank you."

Madeline stared at him and managed a smile, "I…I don't know what to say. Well, actually, I do. This is incredible and wonderful and thank you. Thank you from the bottom of my heart." She put her hand on Jonah's and stared into his eyes, "You…you are very generous."

Jonah handed her a business card, "Call my lawyer, who will advise you as to tax strategies before you deposit it."

Madeline and Jonah's lunch was relatively short. After forty minutes, Jonah stood up, kissed Madeline on the cheek three times, Gallic style, paid the bill, and left for the airport. He never had been much of a talker.

Madeline went to Coda Gems.

She took Jonah's check out of her wallet and handed it to Abby. "This is the reward Jonah Musgrave gave me for finding the jewels and then leaving them with him, ensuring they would end up with the Pasteur Institute."

Abby stared at the check, and after a very long pause, she looked up, "Sorry, Madeline, I had to count the zeroes a couple of times."

Which was as close to making a joke about money as Abby had ever come.

"Since we don't have to sell Coda Gems," said Madeline, "we can make big plans now with our reward money and…"

"It's your reward money," Abby pointed out.

"No, it's our reward money. We are partners, and it's the right thing to do. I know this money will help us be very successful." insisted Madeline.

Abby paused for a long minute and then said, "Yes, of course, we will be very successful."

"There is one thing," said Madeline, "I will want to take out money from our reward to make an immediate personal purchase. I need to buy a ruby ring for Shay right away, Burmese, of course, a big Burmese ruby ring."

"That's an excellent idea," and Abby smiled and then laughed until she had tears in her eyes. The two partners stood and hugged, and then left for dinner at *Aujord'hui'* at the Four Seasons. At dinner Abby proposed a toast to Jonah, and then they took turns toasting him until they nearly finished two bottles of champagne.

Madeline did go to New Hampshire with Felix for a long weekend five days later. After they returned, Madeline was unpacking when Shay walked in her bedroom.

"How was your trip to New Hampshire with Felix?" asked Shay.

"It was beautiful, wonderful, and fabulous, and not to beat a tired adjective to death, it was 'spectacular.' We went on two incredible hikes in the White Mountains, and then we had a very long dinner at the 1902 Restaurant at Bretton Woods, and we talked and talked and…"

"And? asked Shay, "and then? Then what happened?"

"You mean later? Back in our room?" and Shay nodded. Madeline continued, "Well…the earth moved under my feet," she said with a slow smile.

Shay knew what she meant. She said, "I am glad to hear that, but what will happen next? I want to know before I fly back to San Francisco. Tell me, you must tell me."

"I don't know, we're just 'together' now, and that's enough."

"For now," said Shay.

"Yes, for now," Madeline said.

"Well," said Shay. "I am glad you finally came to your senses. But what do you think will happen after that?"

"I don't know, anything could happen."

"Anything?" pressed Shay.

Madeline said with a slow smile, "Yes," she said, "anything can happen, anything. Who knows what will happen?"

Acknowledgements

I would like to thank Verena Rose, Shawn Simmons, and Deb Well of Level Best Books for their dedication to the fine art of crime fiction, as well as Pam Mayer, a talented graphic designer.

About the Author

Mary E. Stibal has never considered 'less is more' a virtue, especially when it comes to gems. (Think Mrs. Simpson.) Mary has also long known that beautiful gems are a stone-cold motive for any manner of crime. Especially murder. So using her decades-long business background, Mary weaves stories of the deadly confluence of Boston's super-rich and their breathtaking jewels with blinding ambition and murder into The Gemstone Mysteries.

https://www.levelbestbooks.us/mary-stibal.html

Also by Mary E. Stibal

A Widow in Pearls

An Ex-Heiress in Emeralds